Math Troubles

Rosalyn Marie Francis

ISBN:0986875988
ISBN-13:9780986875984

DEDICATION

To Philip, my husband, for all his love and support.

ACKNOWLEDGMENTS

Thank you to B. Heather Mantler
my publisher at Lit-N-Laughter
and Sarah Dahlmann for their help in producing this book.

CHAPTER 1

The buzzer to end recess interrupts my daydream but I welcome it. "One more hour of work, and then lunch," I whisper as I enter the classroom and slip into my desk. "An afternoon of games in the gym and then a whole week of no school..." I squeeze my eyes shut; the rest is too good to even to whisper.

"What's wrong?" Someone touches my shoulder.

I open my eyes and smile at my best friend, Serena, "Just thinking about spring break."

Serena lets out a sigh, "A whole boring week of Mom making me do housework." My forehead wrinkles as I watch my friend's eyes shift toward the front of the room. I follow her eyes but all I see is our teacher, Mr. Richter. He surveys the class for a minute before rapping his ruler against the side of the desk.

"Class, take your seats." Serena instantly obeys and sits straight up with her hands clasp on the desktop.

I straighten up in my seat to look attentive as the teacher stands to his feet. "I thought we would do something different for the last class before the break. We're going to do our math problems on the board today. To give it an extra challenge, if the entire class gets their questions right then, I won't give you homework over spring break. If on the other hand, students get their question wrong you will do the rest of the chapter on word problems and there will be a unit test the first period back. To make it easier we'll split the class into two teams, teammates will be able to help the person doing the problem by shouting out the next step. Serena and Russell will be the team captains. Serena's team along that wall and Russell's team over here."

Serena and Russell leave their desks to take their places at the front of the room. Mr. Richter pauses. "Now to see who picks first. Team captains only, please. What is one hundred and twenty-five divided by zero?"

Russell speaks first. "Zero."

The teacher pauses then glances toward Serena. "Serena, what is one hundred and twenty-five divided by zero."

Serena hesitates for a minute then glances at Joe, who is the class math whizz. Finally, she says. "You can't divide anything by zero."

"Serena is right, anything divided by zero is undefined. Serena picks first."

Russell frowns but says nothing, which doesn't stop a whisper behind me. "Unfair, trick question."

I lean back in my seat with full knowledge that Serena would choose me for her team. Serena glances toward me. She pauses and then she says. "Joe."

Joe sticks his pencil behind his ear and walks up to stand beside Serena. Okay, I admit Joe is the best math student in the class. I sigh and wait to be her next choice.

Russell picks Toby, his best friend, no surprise there.

Serena takes the longest second of my life then calls "Barbara." My cheeks flame. She already had her expert. You'd think it was a competition the way she picked another good math student.

Before Russell can choose again, Toby leans over and whispers in his ear. Russell smiles before calling out. "Abby."

Startled, it takes me a moment to recognize my name; finally, with everyone staring at me I rise from my seat. As I walk toward the front of the room, Serena frowns at me. What can I do but shrug my shoulders? Toby leers at me so I leave a large gap between us.

Toby snickers in a whisper. "Scared of boy germs?" I glance at the teacher who frowns in the direction of the noise but turns his attention back to Serena as she calls out the next name. "We'll see how smart girls really are." Toby scoffs in a whisper. I clasp my hands together to stop them from shaking.

Serena calls "Becky." Russell pauses. "Steve." Steve walks up right behind me and shoves me with his hand on the side away from the teacher. I stagger a step towards Toby. "Get in line," Steve orders in a whisper. Mr. Richter turns and frowns at me. Toby snickers again.

As the two captains continue to call out names, Serena picks the girls, and Russell chooses the boys.

Finally, Mr. Richter goes to the board and writes out a word problem. "Serena, you go first. For this to be fair, Russell's team has to be silent while Serena's team works on their problems and I expect Serena's team to be silent when Russell's team has its turn."

Serena smiles sweetly at Mr. Richter then picks up the chalk. She reads the problem aloud then does the first step of the problem before glancing towards Joe. Joe either nods or shakes his head and she continues or erases the last step. Finally, she writes the last number and steps back.

"That's correct." Mr. Richter smiles, "Russell, it's your turn."

Russell picks up the chalk and then he turns his attention to the board and works out the problem ignoring the calls of help from behind him. He holds out the chalk to Mr. Richter.

"Good job, Russell." Mr. Richter takes the chalk and writes the next problem out before handing the chalk to Joe.

Joe glances at the chalk. "The answer is fifty-six point seventy-five. Do I have to write out the steps?"

"I guess not." Mr. Richter erases the problem and replaces it with the next one. "Toby?"

Toby takes the chalk and walks jauntily to the board. "Now give me all the help you can, boys and Ab-i-gail."

My face reddens at his sassy use of my hated first name. The boys get fully involved calling out every step of the process. Finally, Toby steps back and tosses the chalk to Mr. Richter. "That's right, isn't it?"

"With enough help, you managed to get it right." The teacher cups his hands to catch the chalk.

Toby takes his seat at the back of the room.

The next question goes up on the board and Barbara gets the chalk. She ignores all her teammates and their attempts at assistance but she goes an extra step and does the question backwards to prove her answer before admitting to being finished.

"You better not mess up." Steve whispers and shoves me. "I don't want to do no homework or math test."

I take the chalk from the teacher and my fingers feel like unbending sticks. The chalk falls from my fingers; it seems like forever as I watch it fall to the ground where until it shatters into pieces on the concrete floor. My heart pounds as I bend down to retrieve the shattered pieces while the entire class watches. Choosing the longest pieces I set them on the metal ledge beneath the blackboard before I try to scrape the crumbled bits together and pick them off the floor. I take extra time to walk them to the wastebasket while everyone waits.

I choose the biggest piece of chalk off the ledge then step back to whisper the problem to myself. I am halfway through when Steve pipes up. "Get on with it, A-bi-ga-il." He manages to stretch my name out twice as long as Toby had. I try to ignore him then he starts. "Thirteen…"

Toby interrupts him from the back of the room. "Give her a chance to solve it for herself."

Steve falls silent. I don't even hear the rustle of paper in the room. A prickle runs up my spine as the silence of the room settles on my shoulders. I feel my shoulders rise slightly to fend off the heaviness. I feel every eye in the class on my back. I try to read the board but it is like the letters and numbers transform into a random series of chalk lines that float on my tears. I blink and try to read it again but my eyes water turning the whole thing into a mess of blurry white marks. My muscles tighten up and I want to run but the weight on my shoulders kept me anchored to the floor.

"Abby?" Mr. Richter asks.

"I can't do it." I whisper. A great sadness washes threw me.

"Russell, she needs your teams help. Get them to help her."

"Okay, come on guys." Russell urges them.

Suddenly a dozen voices rise as twelve different sets of instructions crash over me. The sadness turns to panic as the voices drown out what control I have. I turn and yell at the whole class. "Shut up! I can't think!"

The room instantly quietens. I turn back to look at the problem. I try to blink back the tears that block my vision as I try harder to make the mass of squiggles make sense. Suddenly the unfairness of it all floods me, Serena should have picked me, and the teacher should have stopped the boys from teasing me and using my awful first name. The red in my cheek rise and block my vision as anger replaces the out of control feeling of moments earlier.

Mr. Richter frowns. "Abigail!"

"Don't call me that, I'm Abby." I slam the piece of chalk into the ledge. "I can't do your dumb problem!" I go to my seat and flop down. I fold my arms across my chest and stare straight ahead.

"Abigail, go to the principal's office, right now."

As swiftly as it came, my anger deserts me. I rise from my chair and head for the door; I want out of there before I burst into tears in front of the whole class. I am still fighting back tears when I reach the office. The secretary looks up. "What?"

"Mr. Richter sent me to the principal's office." I announce. The first tear trickles down my face so I brush it away with the back of my hand. "My name is Abby Hansen."

"Take a seat. I will tell the principal that you are here." The woman gives me a half-hearted smile.

Thoughts rush through my mind, it wasn't fair. Dad's voice interjects. "Abby, life is unfair, you have to do the best with what you have." I release a deep sigh. Dad won't accept me getting mad and being sent to the principal just because things didn't turn out my way. Dad wouldn't have let the boys get to him. Dad works hard, he runs his own business. Dad said if everything went well we could go visit the royal museum and see the dinosaurs during spring break. The museum had another name but it was too long to remember I just knew it was a special place because it was royal.

Another great sadness wells up in me. Things hadn't gone well, now we wouldn't go. I should have done the math problem. I should have been able to ignore the boys and done the problem then everything would be better. I sigh even deeper, I wasn't going to get to go at all because I couldn't do math. There was something wrong with me, everyone could do math except Toby, and he couldn't because he didn't want to work. I often heard him and Russell talking behind me during class. Toby was saving his brain for better things. Or so he said. No, I was a bad person who couldn't do math. More tears escape so I didn't notice when the woman stop by my chair. I didn't look up until she spoke.

"I am Ms. Shelby, the principal. Are you Abby?"

I look up and nod.

"What is the matter?"

A possible solution pops into my head so I ask. "Can I get transferred to another school?"

"I think, maybe, you should come into my office." The principal leads the way into a room, offers me a tissue and a chair then waits while I wipe my face and blow my nose.

"Tell me why you want to change schools?"

I take a deep breath and test my theory. "I can't do math anymore."

"To my knowledge, all grade fives take math in every school." The principal frowns and then turns and types something into the computer then reads a screen I couldn't see. Ms. Shelby pauses. "You got a B in math on the last report card."

"I didn't mind math until today, but now I can't do it." The words burst from me and rush out.

There is a short silence. "Tell me what happened in class today."

"The teacher made us do math problems on the board. Mr. Richter broke us into teams. I ended up on the boy's team because Serena picked all the good math students instead of me. I couldn't do my problem, now they will all hate me." My voice drops to a whisper.

"Why would they hate you for having trouble with a math problem?"

"Mr. Richter said that if everyone got the problems right then, we wouldn't have any homework over the break; but, if anyone got their question wrong, we'd have to finish the chapter and do a test the first day back after spring break." My eyes flood with tears. "The boys blame me 'cause now they have to do math homework and a test."

Ms. Shelby releases a long breath. "I must talk to Mr. Richter. Please wait out on the chair in the outer office?"

I nod and slip off my chair when my other grievance springs to mind. "Mr. Richter called me Abigail. I told him not to; but, he and the boys do it anyways."

"Abigail is a nice name."

"Abigail is my birth mother's name. My dad says I'm an individual, I'm Abby. Could you tell him not to call me Abigail anymore?"

Ms. Shelby nods in answer. "I will tell him."

I go back to the chair in the outer office. I think about math and what not being able to do math would mean. Dad lets me help him with the grocery shopping. It is my job to take a calculator and add up everything as we pick things off the shelf. Dad asks for running totals as we go down the aisles. Sometimes I mix muffins, Dad once pointed out I needed to know fractions to read the measuring cups. Fractions are math. Dad likes my muffins. A tear runs down my face as I think about never making baking again. I guess I sort of know when Mr. Richter passes me to go into Ms. Shelby's office and then he comes out again later but everything is blurry through my tears.

Ms. Shelby comes out of her office. "Abby, you can go back to class now. Mr. Richter has changed his mind about giving that math homework and test now." The buzzer rings. "There will be no more math class for today,"

I return to the classroom where kids are taking their lunches from a side shelf. I stop to get my lunch on the way to my seat.

Serene shoves me aside then grimaces at me. "Mr. Richter might quit because of you."

I glance at my backpack on the shelf but my stomach feels heavy rather than hungry. I go to my desk, fold my arms and lay my head on my arms. I am still there when the lunch monitor comes around. "Everybody it's time to be outside."

I rise and go to the bathroom. A bunch of chattering girls hush as I enter the bathroom. There is a snicker after I close the stall door. I listen for them to leave before I step out of the enclosure to wash my face and hands.

The lunch monitor sticks her head into the washroom. "You should be outside."

I don't want to go outside and face Serena so I lie. "I don't feel well."

"Then I'd better take you down to the office. Come along." The woman instructs before leading the way.

The secretary pauses at her second visit from me that

day. "Not having a good day, I see."

"I've got to get out to the playground." The monitor walks away.

"What is the problem?"

"My stomach hurts." I speak, and then realize it is the truth.

"Is there an adult at home?"

I nod. "Dad's office is in the basement. He is usually there."

"I will call him." The woman opens a drawer and flips through some files until she opens one. "Maybe he can come and get you. There are no real classes this afternoon so there is no work for you to miss." She picks up the phone. The secretary waits for a few minutes then she speaks. "This is Banks Elementary School if Ted Hansen could call the school office concerning his daughter." She hangs up the receiver, "Answering machine."

"He probably has a client in his office." I wrap my arms around my stomach. "He puts the answering machine on so they won't be disturbed."

"Hopefully, he will call soon," The secretary smiles. "You can sit here or you can lie down in the first aid room."

"I'll sit here."

I am there for some time before the principal walks in. "I have to get a few things for the games this afternoon is there anything you need?" Ms. Shelby asks the secretary. The secretary motions toward me. The principal turns then smiles.

"More troubles, Abby?"

"Stomach problems," The secretary says. "As soon as her dad phones back, I was going to let her go home."

"Is he not home?" Ms. Shelby frowns.

"His answering machine picked up the call. Abby said

he sometimes puts the machine on if he is busy."

"You think he's home?" Ms. Shelby turns to me.

"He works from an office in the basement. He rarely goes out."

Ms. Shelby hesitates. "I could give you a ride home; if you are certain, he will be there."

"I am."

"Then go get what you need to take home for the holidays. Remember to take your gym strip to be washed."

Hearing my own footsteps echo in the empty hall sends shivers up my spine. The sound of other children playing outside seems distant. I enter the classroom and gather my gym strip. I put the novel study that is due when we get back in my backpack then add my math textbook. I turn my back to the door while I slip out of my indoor shoes and into my outdoor shoes.

"What are you doing in here?" A deep voice echoes in the empty room.

I spring around to find Mr. Richter standing in the doorway. The intercom buzzes. "Abby is going home sick." Ms. Shelby's voice interrupts. "Are you almost ready to go, Abby?"

"I-I'm just changing my shoes."

"Meet me at the main doors." Ms. Shelby instructs.

I quickly finish changing shoes then grab my coat, backpack and gym strip. I have to stop short of the door as Mr. Richter stands in the way.

"Please, may I get past?"

He frowns. "We wouldn't want you to have to face your classmates, would we?" He says before moving aside.

I stare at him for a second before rushing past.

"Here." I point out a split-level home on a dead end street. Ms. Shelby pulls into the driveway. She opens her car door and steps out.

"You don't have to come in. I have a key." I speak up as I shut the car door.

"I have to make certain your father is home. I would get in trouble if I left you without adult supervision." She answers.

"Oh." I lead the principal around the house to the kitchen door. I unlock it using my key. "Come down to the office to talk to Dad." I stop and lock up behind us.

Ms. Shelby follows me down a short flight of stairs and into an open area. Dad is sitting a computer while a woman in a lacy white blouse with a tailored skirt hovers with her nose poked over his shoulder.

"Ted, I want something that will appeal to kids."

"I have run it by a dozen teenagers…" Dad turns toward the woman and pushes his chair back to move away from her.

"Not teenagers, pre-teens." The woman places her hands on her hips. "I want a site for pre-teen girls, our second largest customer group. I want it online yesterday."

"My contract says every change costs extra and delays the start-up date by a reasonable amount of time to get the job done."

"The new product line comes out this afternoon!"

"This is the site that Bill ordered. If you're changing the requirements, then that's your call, but you're required by contract to give me two weeks."

"It has to be sooner than that if you want any recommendations out of me."

"Finishing it in a week means it will cost extra because

I would be working twenty-four hours a day. There are significant hours of programming and animation involved in a site like this one." Dad leans back in his chair.

"I have a list of websites that are similar to I want. You could just revamp…"

Dad interrupts her. "I don't rip off other designers. My sites are one of a kind which is what your partner ordered. Our deal is my one-of-a-kind sites to match his one-of-a-kind products. I suggest you go talk to your partner. The bill for this website is due and payable in full the minute you break my contract."

The two seem to glare at each other for a long time. I reach out my arm to stop Ms. Shelby from interrupting. "Bill knows nothing…"

"Shall we phone him and see if he agrees with you?" Dad asks softly. The woman blinks.

"I want a site suitable for pre-teen girls and I want it up on the servers by next Friday." She stamps her foot then catches sight of Ms. Shelby out of the corner of her eye. "Who…?"

Dad turns and sees me, "Abby-girl, who's your friend?"

"This is the principal of my school, Ms. Shelby. She brought me home."

I pause. "This is my dad."

"Mr. Hansen." Ms. Shelby is slow to hold out her hand.

"Ted." He corrects as he shakes hands with her. "And this is Miranda Nessman."

Ms. Shelby nods vaguely to acknowledge Miranda then turns to Dad. "Abby had a bad morning in math class, and now her stomach is upset. I needed to verify that she has adult supervision." Ms. Shelby stops. "Sorry to interrupt your meeting."

My stomach squeezes together. Now Dad would ask about everything. He would be disappointed in me and nix the visit to the museum.

"It was good of you to see her home. Abby, can you see Ms. Shelby out? We will talk later." Dad answers before turning back to Miranda. "I better look at your ideas before I waste any more time on this."

I lead Ms. Shelby back upstairs. "Your dad does know that spring break is next week?"

"I marked it on his calendar." I speak quietly. "He checks it every morning."

Ms. Shelby gives me a half-smile. "You will be all right?"

I nod. "Dad will talk to me after his client leaves." I open the door for her.

"Okay, have a good holiday," Ms. Shelby smiles and leaves.

CHAPTER 2

Before I forget, I take my gym strip into the laundry room off the kitchen and toss my t-shirt, shorts and socks in the washing machine. I pull enough other clothes out of the hamper to make up a load and start the washing machine. Not knowing how late Dad would be, I carry the rest of my stuff upstairs. Taking my math and novel study books out of my backpack, I place them on my desk. Slowly I shuffle them until the math text is on top. I open it to the word problems that had been last night's homework. The words and numbers blur and run together. I slam shut the book. Fresh tears run down my cheeks, it was just as I thought I would never be able to do math again. I crawl onto my bed and turn my face into the pillow to cry.

I wake up warm. It takes a minute to realize Dad must have come up and covered me with a blanket. I rub my eyes and slide off the bed. Somehow I am drawn back to the desk where the offending book still sits. I stare at it for a long minute, I almost step that way but suddenly there is an urgent need to go to the bathroom so I head across the hall instead.

I am returning to my room when Dad calls up the stairs. "Abby, I want to talk to you for a few minutes."

I enter the kitchen where Dad is cooking dinner. "What is it, Dad?"

"Sorry Abby-girl, we can't leave this week as planned." Dad turns to glance at me from where he is stirring macaroni and cheese in a saucepan. I know it is my fault. "Come sit down. Serena phoned, she said you can't go to her house for the weekend." I have already figured that one out.

"I have plenty of homework to keep me busy. The teacher said we have a math test on the first Monday back and I'm having a little trouble."

"Call Roland and get him to tutor you. I'll pay him ten dollars an hour." Dad picks up the saucepan to dish up supper out onto two plates. I want you to know Dad does cook other things but he falls back on kd whenever he is working. One plate is set in front of me. He picks up the other plate. "I'll be downstairs." I guess the silent treatment is better than a lecture.

I nod to show that I hear him. Call Serena's brother, a sick feeling enters my stomach as I stir the pasta around on my plate. Then I realize that Roland will want to spend his week off with his friends so I reach for the phone. A quick glance at the clock tells me that I would not be disturbing Roland's supper. I quickly push the buttons on the telephone before I lose my nerve.

It rings once, twice, "Martins residence."

"Mrs. Martins, this is Abby."

"I'll call Serena."

"No, I need to talk to Roland. Is he there?" I snatch a

deep breath.

"Certainly," Mrs. Martins hesitates. "I'll call him." The line goes dead.

"What is it, Abby?"

"I need a math tutor. Dad says he'll pay you for tutoring me." I rush through the explanation.

"How much?"

"Five dollars an hour," I suggest.

"Eight is minimum wage." Roland answers.

"Eight then," I counter then throw in a, "Please." so no one can accuse me of making a bad job of asking.

The line is silent for a few seconds. "Alright, but only for a couple hours a day, say between nine and eleven in the morning."

"See you tomorrow." I agree and hang up the phone with a hollow feeling in my stomach, I turn back my supper. I take one bite. Suddenly I am hungry enough to finish the plate.

Dad comes back upstairs. "Did I hear you on the phone?"

"I phoned Roland. He'll be here at nine in the morning." I answer.

Reaching for the fruit bowl on the counter, Dad holds it out to me. "Pick your dessert."

I hesitate only slightly before choosing a banana. Dad picks out an apple. "Okay, but you work in the kitchen with him."

"I will." I agree as I peel the first third of the banana.

"Off to bed at eight-thirty, I will try to remember to come up and tuck you in." Dad leans down and kisses my forehead. "You can watch a movie until then if you want."

"I need to get started on my homework." I answer.

"Okay." Dad takes his apple and goes back

downstairs.

I finish my banana and go to the laundry room to throw the load with my gym strip into the dryer. I set the time and push the start button before heading upstairs to my room.

My math book tries to draw me when I enter the bedroom, but I decide that other homework is just as important, so I pick up my novel study book. I read the next chapter and then answer the questions. When I finish, I start on the next chapter.

My alarm goes off at eight the next morning, I know Dad will get upset if I am not bathed and dressed before Roland arrives. I choose a plain t-shirt and clean blue jeans. Dad can get fussy about clothes but his favourite word on the subject is decent. I take my math book, paper and pencil downstairs with me. My stomach growls, checking the cupboard, I find we were out of cereal. Without thinking, I take bowls and measuring spoons from the cabinets. By the time Roland arrives, I am pulling freshly baked muffins from the oven.

"You didn't say breakfast was offered."

I consider this seriously. "I have to take some down to Dad but you can have a couple."

"Abby, I'm teasing."

Shrugging, I put three muffins on a plate and take them downstairs. Dad sits in front of the computer with a cup of coffee at his elbow. "Here." I set the food by the coffee cup.

"Good morning." Her father greets me then hugs me. "How are things going?"

I notice his eyes have red lines around the coloured part. "Roland is here."

"How long is he staying?"

"Until eleven," I answer.

"I will check on you later." Dad warns as he picks up a muffin. "You turned the oven off and you won't use it again without telling me first."

"I turned it off." I sigh. "And yes, I'll remember to ask permission next time."

"Good, go work on that math," Dad smiles. I go up to where Roland waits.

Roland is looking through my textbook. "What do you want to start with?"

"Word problems," I answer. "What did Serena say about yesterday?"

"Serena didn't say anything." Roland frowns. "Dad got so sick of hearing about the wonderful Mr. Richter that he refused to listen to her say anything."

I decide to tell him the truth. "I messed up a word problem on the board yesterday. I embarrassed myself in front of the whole class."

"Alright, start at the beginning of the chapter on word problems." Roland flips some pages.

I look at the page where Roland holds the book open. The letters have broken into sticks and arcs which are swimming about on the page.

"Now, find a clean page." Roland instructs.

I put a clean paper in front of me and take a deep breath before looking at the page again. The words and number still run together so I close my eyes then open them again. I know this isn't normal. I'd read a whole two chapters of the novel and answered questions last night. Roland seems to be waiting for me to do something. When I don't start the question, Roland does.

"Mrs. Murphy bakes pies to sell at the farmer's market. She bakes three-dozen peach pies, five-dozen apple pies and six-dozen blueberry pies. The pies are sold both as whole pies and pieces. She cuts the pies she sells into eight pieces, which she sells for seventy-five cents apiece. The whole pies she sells for six dollars apiece. Does she make more, on the pies, or the cut-up pieces? If she sold three pies of each kind cut into pieces and the other pies whole how much money does she make?"

I think about it for a minute. "So they want to know if eight times seventy-five cents is more or less than six dollars."

"That's right." Roland smiles for the first time. "Do the multiplication."

"Eight times five is forty, write down the zero, carry the four. Eight times seven is fifty-six plus four is sixty. The answer is six dollars. All the pies are sold for the same price."

"Okay, if all the pies are six dollars, how much money will she make if she sells all the pies?"

"How many dozen are there?" I ask when I realize I don't remember the first part of the question.

"Three dozen peach pies, five dozen apple pies and six dozen blueberry pies." Roland rereads it.

"Three plus five is eight. Eight plus six is fourteen dozen. A dozen is twelve so fourteen times twelve." I write down the numbers in tidy rows. "Two times four is eight; two times one is two. One times four is four and one times one is one. Eight plus zero is eight, two plus four is six and the one comes down, so there are one hundred and sixty-eight pies."

"There's one more calculation."

"One hundred and sixty-eight pies times six dollars." I nod in agreement. "Six times eight is forty-eight, put down the eight carry the four. Six times six is thirty-six plus four is forty, put down the zero, carry the four again. Six times one is six plus the four is ten. The answer is one thousand and eight dollars in gross sales."

"Okay. You got that one right. Let's go on to the next one." Roland hesitates for a few seconds then starts to read the next question to me. We worked that way for three-quarter of an hour before Dad comes upstairs.

"So, how's the math going?"

Roland's brow wrinkles. "Mr. Hansen, can we discuss this privately?"

Dad glances at Roland and nods. "Come downstairs. Abby, could I get you to water the flowers in the back yard? It's on my list of things to do but I'm not going to get there today."

I leave my math books on the table and go outside. The hose is hooked up so I only have to drag it over to the flowerbed and turn it on to a trickle. I wait and move it every few minutes. It's a long job but I don't mind the time way from my math. The flowers are just coming up, I bend down to count the leaves, most of the plants only have three or four leaves. It would take a few more weeks before they bloom.

The backdoor opens and Roland comes out. "Your Dad says that's enough for one day. See you around Abby."

I glance up. "Bye." I know it is lame but I couldn't think of anything else to say. Tears start to fill my eyes; Dad doesn't think a tutor is any use. He must have guessed how faulty I am. I am sure of it when I go back into the house and my math books are gone. I go to my room and cry quietly into my pillow for a long time. Finally, I get up, wash my face, and go downstairs.

The first thing Dad asks when he comes up to make supper was. "Why did you dicker Roland down to eight bucks an hour? I said ten."

I sigh another mistake. "You always dicker."

Dad stares at me for a moment. "I usually negotiate; but only with people who can afford it."

"Oh!" A lump appears in my stomach. "I didn't know I wasn't supposed to dicker."

"Next time I'll make it clearer." Dad sighs. "Why don't you tear up some lettuce for a salad?"

I nod and go to the refrigerator for the lettuce. Dad is trying to make me feel useful. The salad is nearly done when the phone rings. Dad sets the pan off the heat before he picks up the receiver. "Hansen residence."

"Yes, this is Ted Hansen." There is a long silence. "I'm in the middle of making supper, could I call you back in an hour or two?" A short silence, then Dad picks up a pencil and writes something on a pad of paper by the phone. "Seven o'clock. I'll talk to you then." He hangs up the phone.

Dad goes back to cooking without mentioning the phone call. I set plates, cutlery and glasses at their places. Then I put the salad and salad dressing on the table. Dad splits the contents of the pot between the two plates before setting it in the sink and filling it with water. I slip into my seat at the table and place my hands on my lap. Dad sits down and serves us the salad. He eats in silence for a long time. His eyes are on me so I push food around on my plate hoping he won't notice I am not eating.

Dad asks softly. "What happened at school yesterday?"

"I got sent to the principal's office." I admit.

"Why were you sent to the principal's office?" Dad uses a very soft voice, the one he uses when he doesn't want me to know how mad he really is.

I cringe. "I couldn't do a math question."

"Couldn't or wouldn't?" Dad asks as his voice rises slightly.

"I couldn't read it. Then everyone yelled at me." Tears form in my eyes. "I can't do math anymore."

"How would everyone know? And what makes you think you can't do math?" Dad frowns. "Roland said you had no problems with the math."

"The teacher made us do our math on the chalkboard in front of everyone. I couldn't do mine." I explain. "I couldn't understand the question."

Dad sighs. "What did the principal say?"

"Ms. Shelby said a teacher couldn't make the whole classes do homework and a test because I couldn't do one question on the board. She called Mr. Richter into the office and talked to him."

"Wait a minute, what was this about a test?" Dad frowns.

The words start to tumble out of me so fast. "Mr. Richter said that we had to do problems on the board and if anyone got theirs wrong then the whole class would get homework and then have to write a test the first class back after spring break. I told the principal that everyone would be mad because I made them take a test. Ms. Shelby said that she would stop Mr. Richter from giving everyone a test just because I couldn't do the question."

"So, she objected to the test because of the way he was going about it?"

I sigh but nod. "I also asked her to stop him from calling me Abigail again. Toby called me that first. I told the teacher I didn't like being called that name but then Mr. Richter called me it."

"Finish eating your dinner." Dad sighs. "I'm sure by the time you get back to school everyone will have forgotten about it."

I start to argue then realize that he doesn't understand. Dad raises his left eyebrow and glances at my plate. The lead feeling in my stomach grows worse but I force myself to chew and swallow every bite of the food.

Dad watches me eat the last bite before gathering the dishes. "I think you have done enough homework for today. Watch TV or a movie, I have work to do."

I know this is his way of trying to make me feel better so I give him a quick hug and quickly go upstairs where I throw up my supper in the toilet. Afterwards, I rinse my mouth, wash my face, put on pyjamas and go to bed. Dad loves me but he doesn't understand.

A giant with hands like hams blocks my way out of the room. Here you are! A very deep voice roars. I scream in recognition. My eyes pop open. I am sitting up in bed. Every muscle in my body shakes with fear. A few short seconds later strong arms encase me, the smell of Dad hits me and the fear vanishes although the shaking is only starting to subside as my tears begin to flow.

"Abby, what happened?"

Relief floods me with his solid presence. "I had a nightmare." I lean against his chest. "Grandfather was in my bedroom blocking the doorway."

Dad runs his hand over my hair. "Why don't you come down to the office and sit with me a while until you settle down?" He reaches over to snag a blanket to wrap around me. Dad lifts me out of bed to carry me downstairs.

I cuddle into his chest until he sets me in his second office chair.

"Abby, have you seen your mother or your grandfather anywhere lately?" Dad asks crouching in front of me.

I shake my head, "Just in my nightmare."

"As important as this contract is, I'll chuck it and we'll

go if you are afraid they will find you."

I reach out and brush his bangs back from his forehead. "What's so important about this contract?"

"It could lead to contracts with other businesses, the kind who want the teen websites that I do best. I'm really in over my head with this pre-teen website but if I can do a credible job, then it could mean the company could earn a lot more money."

"Money doesn't matter so much, does it?" I frown.

"It's a hard commodity to live without," Dad answers. "I lived that way long enough to know."

"Then why would you be willing to chuck the contract and just go away?" I rub my eyes maybe my brain was still asleep, I didn't understand.

"None of it matters if you're not happy." Dad manages a half-smile.

"You have to be happy too." I protest. "You've worked hard to get this business going. You can't just quit. I promise I haven't seen grandfather or my mother."

"What about your problems at school?" Dad asks.

"The principal told me that wherever I go there would be math." I sigh. "And as long as I can't do math, I'll be in trouble with the teacher."

Dad frowns. "Why do you believe that math is so hard? Roland said you had no trouble with the math: it was reading the questions that you refused to do."

This is my chance to make Dad understand. I take a deep breath. "When I try to read the questions in the textbook, everything goes blurry and the letters and numbers break down into sticks that float on the page. Just like when I tried to read the question on the board, the harder I try the worse it gets." I frown at the memory.

"This never happened before?" Dad asks. I shake my head. "You were doing this question on the board in front of the whole class?"

I nod. "Have you ever had to do your math on the board before?" I shake my head again. "Were you scared when you started the question?"

"I was upset." I admit. "Serena didn't pick me for her team so I ended up on the boys' team."

"Then what happened?"

"The boys teased me and called me Ab-i-ga-il. When I tried the question, it got all disjointed and blurry. Everyone yelled at me, I got mad and told Mr. Richter I couldn't do the dumb problem. That's when Mr. Richter called me Abigail and sent me to the principal's office." I slump in the chair.

"You were upset then you panicked and your brain used all its resources to deal with the emergency so you had no ability to think about the question. It happens to everyone occasionally." Dad informs me. "Except now when you look at the textbook your brain remembers how you felt looking at the board and goes into panic."

"How do I stop it?" I ask.

"That, unfortunately, takes a wiser head than mine." Dad sags a little. His hand comes up to rub his eyes. "I promise to get you some help but it's going to have to wait until I finish this project."

I tighten the blanket around myself. Suddenly the thought that Dad can't handle everything registers in my brain. A cold fear grabs a corner of my heart.

"Dad, are you all right?" I feel the tremble in my voice.

Dad pauses, and then tries to smile but the corners of his lips only raise a fraction of an inch. "I could use some help down here. I know nothing about websites for pre-teen girls. Any suggestions about what you or your friends might like."

"What's the website for?" I ask.

"Since the product has hit the market and is no longer top secret," Dad moves to his own chair and sits down. "I can show you."

CHAPTER 3

I wake the next morning to birds singing outside the window. Somehow a happy feeling causes me to smile, maybe with my ideas Dad will get the website done. Then I get out of bed and notice that my math textbook is back on my desk. Somehow the idea takes root in my mind that if I could read the math problems, everything else would be all right. I move to stand in front of the book, I close my eyes and form a wish what I whisper to myself. I reach out and flip the book open in the middle. Little sticks and arcs are scattered in no particular order across the page I slam the front cover back down and sit on the bed releasing a long sigh.

A quick knock on the door distracts my attention. Dad sticks his head in. "Shower and get dressed, you have Sunday school."

"Serena's mad at me. She thought Mr. Richter was going to quit because of me." I blink as I realize what Dad had said. "How did you know I go to Sunday school with them?"

"Your Sunday school teacher phoned to get my permission for you to attend the class months ago. Technically I am your father and do have to be consulted," Dad grimaces, "Even if Serena's parents think otherwise."

"But-" I start.

"Since you stayed home this weekend and I need a break from that website, I am taking you."

My mouth sags open. "You don't go to church!"

Dad stares at me for a moment. "My daughter thinks I am a complete pagan. I guess it is time I went. I will put cold cereal on the table."

"We're all out of cereal." I inform him.

"Then I will go mix pancakes, take a few extra minutes in the shower. Now get ready to go." Dad answers and shuts the door.

I glance nervously at Dad and cling to his hand as he opens the church door and ushers me into the building. "Where does your Sunday School class meet?"

"We sit during the singing part of the service before they call all the kids forward for a blessing and then we go down to class as a group." I inform him. "I could..."

"We need to find a seat in the service." Dad leads me in the direction of the double doors. "Show me where."

Mr. Baker hands Dad a folded bulletin. "You're new here."

"My daughter, Abby, has been coming for a while. I'm Ted Hansen."

"Willy Baker. Come with me I'll find you a seat." The man leads us to a pew with open space.

"Mr. Hansen, Abby," Roland comes over. "Good morning." He holds out his hand and Dad shakes it. "I'd sit with you but the sound man is training me to be his helper."

"We will do fine on our own," Dad smiles.

"You know anyone else who comes here?"

"I wouldn't know." Dad admits.

"Dad and Mom are sitting over there." Roland points across the aisle. Serena meets my eyes across the aisle and then deliberately turns her back. I stiffen before I feel Dad's hand on my shoulder.

"See you then." Roland smiles and heads toward the back of the church. Serena's mother waves from across the aisle. Dad acknowledges the wave with a nod of his head.

The worship team enters the sanctuary and takes their places up front. Pastor Ben steps to his place at the microphone. "Shall we open in prayer?"

After we sing a few songs, Pastor Ben calls all the children forward. I give Dad a quick hug and start forward, Serena makes it obvious to anyone with eyes that she isn't walking with or standing by me. Another girl named Hailey, who never talks to Serena, comes up beside me. Hailey smiles and I smile back.

The whole group of us walk out of the sanctuary and down the stairs to where the Sunday school classrooms are located. "Come sit with me." Hailey leads the away into the classroom. Serena chooses a seat on the other side of the circle of chairs.

Miss Penny, our teacher, smiles at everyone. "In today's class, we are going discuss how Jesus dealt with the people he met. We have been reading stories about how Jesus healed the sick, how he forgave people for their sins, and how he told people about a better way to live."

Serena pipes up. "Jesus didn't forgive everyone he called the Pharisees vipers and told people about their faults."

"You are right, but did he speak to them out of love or did he do it out of hate or fear?" Miss Penny asks. The class is silent for a long time so she starts again. "If I see you do a bad thing; is it more loving for me to tell you about it so you can correct it or let you continue to act wrongly and get in serious trouble?"

Hailey puts up her hand. "The woman at the well changed her ways and became a believer after Jesus told her what she had done wrong. She understood Jesus loved her."

"That is true." Miss Penny agrees. "But not everyone, not even all the people Jesus healed became believers. People had to decide to follow Jesus."

I put up my hand. "What does it means to follow Jesus?" I hear Serena snicker across the room but no one joins her.

"Another good question," Miss Penny smiles at me. "Jesus told his disciples or followers to do certain things. The most important one was to love God more than anything else and the next important was to love other people. Loving people is the hardest job, Jesus taught us that it means forgiving their bad actions even when they do them deliberately, helping them when they are having trouble, and being happy with people who are happy, and sad when bad things happen to other people."

"Some people deserve the treatment they get." Serena announces.

"The Bible says that if people really got what they deserve no one would go to heaven." Hailey challenges her. "We would all die. Doesn't it, Miss Penny?"

"The Bible does say that all have sinned and fall short of the glory of God." Miss Penny agrees.

One of the other girls puts up her hand. "Miss Penny,

do we need to help adults too?"

"Sometimes, we all need help sometimes." Miss Penny answers. "Although some people have the gift of healing like Jesus, not everyone can heal people using miracles. We definitely do not know everything that has happened to someone like Jesus did with the woman at the well. What Jesus asks us to do is to help the people we meet whether or not we believe that they did something to deserve their situation or not."

"What if they would do something bad if they caught you?" It is only after the words are out of my mouth that I realize that I said them.

Every eye in the room turns to me. "I mean...like girls who get kidnapped and killed?" I try to correct my mistake.

I look at Miss Penny. Serena pipes up. "You just have to trust God to look after you."

Miss Penny frowns. "Yes, but God gives adults to protect you as well; parents, teachers and family friends. The Bible also says that Jesus did not trust everyone but found a few trustworthy men to carry on his work. He only let himself be arrested after he had talked to God and knew what God wanted him to do."

"My cousin says his Sunday school class goes out to talk to street people about Jesus." Another girl, named Rachel, speaks up. "His parents brag about him." The thought of doing anything like that sends a shiver up my spine.

"How old is your cousin?" Miss Penny asks.

"Fourteen." Rachel answers.

"But he probably goes out with a mixed group of teenagers and adults." Miss Penny emphasizes her last word. "There are some street ministries and some soup kitchens who are always looking for adult and teenaged volunteers. Our class is too young to get involved in that. It might be better to start out smaller and closer to home."

"Mrs. West can always use helpers." Hailey speaks up.

"That is a good suggestion," Miss Penny smiles.

"She smells like mint and moth balls." Serena objects.

"If you were eighty and mostly blind, you would have problems too." Hailey defends her choice.

Miss Penny glances around the room. "Does anyone else know someone who needs help?"

"Do they have to be old?" Serena asks.

"No." Miss Penny shakes her head.

"Abby's father needs help with a website. Roland said so." Serena gives me a sneer.

Miss Penny glances my way. "Abby, do you know what Serena is talking about?"

My cheeks warm. "Dad usually does website for teenagers and he has teenaged guys who come over for what he calls a focus group. Now he has to do a website directed at pre-teen girls. I gave him some ideas last night. I don't know how much more help he needs."

"Wow, that's exciting." Hailey's eyes pop open. "You mean if we helped him our ideas might wind up on the Internet?"

"Better than that, Roland has been in a few focus groups. They get paid." Serena preens.

Miss Penny frowns. "This is not for profit. Serena, we were talking about showing people God's love."

"That doesn't mean he doesn't need the help." Hailey is quick to point out. "Your dad doesn't come to church, does he, Abby?"

"He came today," I pause, "to bring me to Sunday school."

"I vote we ask him if he needs a focus group." Hailey

glances around at the other girls.

"He'll say no, Abby never has other girls over to her house." Serena's tone is sharp. I blush.

Miss Penny notices. "Serena, you are prejudging, whether or not Mr. Hansen would accept our help. All we can do is ask, if he needs and would like our help."

I take a deep breath. I think leave it to Dad. I like that idea.

"I've known Abby for two years and I never got an invitation to her house. I wouldn't plan on this working."

My back stiffens Hailey turns to me and winks. "Maybe your mother turned down the invitation. Your parents prefer you to have friends over instead of allowing you out of her sight. You've never accepted an invitation to my house."

Serena's lips thin, but she holds back what she was going to say.

"We can ask Abby's father after church. Right now we need to get back to the lesson." Miss Penny announces. "What else do we know about Jesus and how he treated people?"

I hardly remember the rest of the class. Dad's possible reaction to being asked absorbs my thoughts. Yesterday I might have said I knew his answer but he came to church this morning. I think about him sitting up there and how after church the elders and the pastor would come up to meet him and ask all kinds of questions.

Don't get me wrong I love my dad and he's usually good with people. I just wish I could be there to protect him from the busybodies, of which Mrs. Martins is the worst. My mother is a touchy subject, and that's the kind of question Mrs. Martins likes to ask. Since we've never discussed church or Sunday school, Dad has no way of knowing that all I say anyone about mom is that she doesn't live with us. Not that they never married, or that Dad asked the judge to sever all ties between her and me, or even that I'm supposed to run the other way at the sight of her.

Not that a lot of adults ask me about her but it's different with kids, except, of course, Serena's mother who asked me lots of questions until I figured out that if I remembered something urgent to do I didn't have to answer. Before then I just mumbled something under my breath and asked about her garden, which was good for a solid half hour of hearing about her unusual roses.

"Abby!" I look up to find Miss Penny frowning at me.

"What?" I blink.

"You are daydreaming, girl." Miss Penny softens her words with a lovely smile. Miss Penny is sweet but young. Serena's mother mutters things about her. Her husband frowns and says something about giving Jesus' grace a chance.

I glance at the other girls but they are all busy writing on papers. Hailey nudges my copy slightly closer without raising her head. I pick it up and read the questions. The first one is about the woman at the well and second about a man born blind that Jesus healed.

"Abby, do you need a pen?" Miss Penny asks.

I nod and stand up to get one out of a jar on the side counter. Miss Penny comes to stand beside me. "Is there anything wrong?"

"No." I shake my head.

Miss Penny just smiles at me. I pick up a pen and go back to where I was sitting. Hailey offers me a smile. I take my seat again.

I start to write the answers on the paper. I haven't finished the first question when Miss Penny announces. "Class is over. Take the questions home and work on the answers. We will discuss them in next week's class."

Folding the paper, I tuck it into my pocket. Hailey grabs my arm. "Let's go find your Dad." The other girls gather around us. Serena lifts her nose.

"I think it might be better if one person talked to Abby's father rather than a mob." Miss Penny interrupts as she gathers pens.

Hailey sends me a pleading look but I didn't get a chance to answer. "Abby, are you ready to go home?" Dad asks from the doorway.

Then the strangest thing happens, Miss Penny drops the pens. The rest of the girls stop in their tracks and stare at Dad. Hailey's mouth drops open but no sound comes out.

"Dad," I start then hesitate. Hailey's eyes beg me to ask. "My Sunday School class would like to volunteer to be your focus group for the website. They heard you need help." I bite my lower lip.

Dad raises one eyebrow. "You told them?"

"Actually no, Serena heard about it from her brother Roland." Miss Penny sounds slightly winded as she stands up. "We were just discussing helping people as Jesus did."

"Ah." Dad nods. "And you are?"

"Dad, this is my Sunday School teacher, Miss Penny." I clear my throat and step into the gap. "Miss Penny, this is my Dad, Ted Hansen. You two talked on the phone."

Glancing back at me, Dad waves me toward him. "Yes, Miss Whitfield."

Miss Penny's cheeks go a pretty pink colour. "I wish you would call me Penny. The girls were really very interested in helping on the website, Mr. Hansen."

"A focus group takes preparation, Miss…Penny. It is not just getting a group of girls together. I have to talk to my client and get him to do a proper introduction to the product so he is assured that this is not just a social visit."

"With spring break, most of the girls would be available all week." Penny frowns.

"Except I have to launch this site by next Friday," Dad answers. "I am facing a very tight deadline."

"Please, Mr. Hansen." Hailey openly pleads. "It would be so exciting; working on something that would go up on the Internet."

Dad sighs. "It would help, wouldn't it Dad?" I ask hoping I am not getting him into something he will hate.

Running his fingers through his hair, a sigh of indecision for my dad, "It would help but the chances of arranging the product education on such short notice is…" Dad breaks off.

"Couldn't you, at least, make some calls?" I feel torn between knowing how Dad hates having people in the house and wanting my classmates over for the afternoon, or, at least, showing them that I was doing my best to make this happen.

Dad takes a deep breath. "I would have to go home to make the calls."

"There is a phone here." Penny offers, "In the church office."

"Even if I thought it was appropriate to make business calls from here, I need the phone numbers which are at home."

Miss Penny blushes. Hailey frowns. "You could make the calls then phone Miss Penny. She could phone us and tell our parents."

"Miss Penny…" Somehow her name sounds different coming from Dad, "might be busy."

"No, I would be willing to act as a go-between. I could even pick the girls up and drop them off." Miss Penny smiles, "I can use my father's van. It has enough seats. That way I can chaperon which I would do for any venture that started in my class."

"You would handle parents and rides?" Dad asks.

Miss Penny nods. "Just call me and tell me what time. I will get as many of the girls as possible there."

"What times are you available, Miss Penny?" Dad asks.

"Late afternoons, every day this week, I work school hours."

"I will try to set it up for an afternoon this week." Dad answers.

"Can it be today, I have got computer camp all week?" Hailey frowns.

"Until I talk to people I have no idea if a focus group is possible which means I need to get out of here." Dad glances at me, "Ready to go."

I nod then pause. "Do you have Miss Penny's phone number?"

Dad laughs. "No, I cannot say I do."

Miss Penny quickly writes something on a slip of paper and gives it to Dad who puts it in the front pocket of his dress shirt. "I will call when I have an answer. Come on, Abby-girl," He places his hand on my head and directs me out of there, "let's get out of here before you get me into anything else."

"Bye." I call out over my shoulder but my stomach sinks, Dad doesn't really want a focus group there I can tell. I sigh, it is all because I can't do math. If I'd done the question we would be visiting with dinosaurs.

"See you later." Hailey answers. I think she has her fingers crossed.

Dad walks me to his car. Willy Baker and another of the elders are standing looking at it. Dad takes out the key.

"Got all the original parts?" Willy Baker asks.

"None has been changed that I know." Dad answers.

"A little fixing up and you could enter this beauty in the classic car rally." The second man says.

"I have neither the time nor the mechanical inclination." Dad opens the back door for me then shuts it after he watches me cinch the seat belt.

The man hands Dad a card. "Call me and we'll talk. It'd be a pity to waste such a vehicle."

Dad glances at the card before putting it in his pocket. "Roger Whitfield. You related to Miss Penny?"

"I'm her father." The man frowns. "How you know Penny?"

"She is Abby's Sunday School teacher. I just met her this morning." Dad gets into the car. "She offered to arrange for her class to help me with a website."

"If Penny said it then she'll do it." Roger Whitfield answers. "Penny thinks the world of her students."

Dad rolls down his window. Mr. Whitfield leans down. "Think about the car, a few adjustments and a little body work is all it would take to triple or quadruple its worth."

"I like my car as it is." Dad starts the engine.

"Think about it. A week or two isn't going to make a lot of difference." Roger smiles, "So long, little lady." He smiles at me then steps back to let Dad safely back away.

"I'm sorry if I embarrassed you by coming to get you." Dad starts before we are entirely out of the parking lot.

"You didn't embarrass me. Parents come and get girls whenever they have to leave right after church. Did you talk to Mrs. Martins?"

"No, was there a reason I should; other than you and Serena are upset with each other?"

I bite my lip. "It's just sometimes she asks a lot of questions. I refused to tell her anything about mom so I thought she might ask you."

"No, but then I left right after the service. It seems I have a lot of work to do." Dad meets my eyes in the rear view mirror.

I bite back my apology about the focus group. If I blink before it happens, Dad will cancel. "How was the service?" I ask to fill the silence that follows his statement.

"About how I remembered," Dad laughs apparently at my expression. "You never knew your old man ever darkened a church doorway."

"Darkened?" I frown.

"Went to church, crossed the doorway of a church." Dad explains.

I wait a while then ask. "When did you go?"

"I had a foster mother who insisted I go to church." Dad grimaces. "I was thirteen that summer."

"Why didn't you keep going to church?" I ask after a few minutes. I usually don't ask questions because Dad doesn't like talking about his past.

"She told me I was passed redemption."

"Passed what?" I frown.

"Saving," Dad answers.

I think about what I had learned in Sunday school. "Nobody's good enough on their own what's why God forgives."

"She decided I was not worth forgiving." Dad pulls into the driveway.

"Then she didn't think very highly of Jesus. He died for the sins of the whole world, and if what wasn't good enough for her then nothing ever will be."

Dad meets my eyes in the rear view mirror. I see a

twinkle that breaks out in a grin. "Abby-girl," I hear him chuckle, "stay an innocent nine forever."

I frown. "I can't, my birthday's coming up."

Dad laughs even harder. I sigh and get out of the car. Dad sometimes asks the impossible. He opens his car door and stands up.

"How about having sandwiches for lunch?"

"What kind?" I turn back to talk to him. I'm not mad just a little frustrated.

"Cheese or canned tuna," He suggests.

"I've had lots of cheese lately,"

Dad grimaces at me. I stick out my tongue at him then pull it back in to say, "Which leaves tuna."

"So long as it is not swimming in mayonnaise," Dad agrees.

"I'll make the sandwiches if you make the phone calls." I offer.

"Abby, how important is this to you?"

I take a deep breath. "Today I was Abby, not Serena's friend, but Abby."

Dad nods before he promises. "I will try to put it together."

I smile "Thanks, Dad." then I start towards the house to the kitchen door.

CHAPTER 4

"Go light on the mayonnaise." He makes it sound like a warning. Just because I overdid the mayonnaise once doesn't mean I will make the same mistake again.

Dad goes downstairs as I get the stuff for the sandwiches. I have them together before he comes back up.

"Everything is arranged. Bill Nessman is coming for three, Miss Penny and your friends are coming for three-thirty and hopefully I will have some ideas by five."

"Will you cut these in half?" I point to the sandwiches. I know Dad won't object because he prefers if I don't use the really sharp knives.

Dad takes the cutting board and the knife and cuts the sandwiches into triangles, which he knows I like. I take glasses out of the cupboard and milk out of the fridge. Dad watches me pour the milk without saying anything, which is an improvement over a few months ago.

We sit down together. "I usually buy the guys pizza as

a reward after a focus group. What do your friends like to eat?"

I think about all the party times we have had in Sunday school. "Ice cream sundaes," I think for a second. "But they like pizza too."

Dad moves his head from side to side for a few seconds then nods. "I think I can do that."

Knowing we didn't have the ice cream or the right kind of cheese for pizza, I pick up my sandwich look at it and say. "We don't have time to go shopping."

"You let me take care of things." Dad looks serious but I see a twinkle in his eye.

I smile and bite into the squishy tuna. Dad does too and groans.

Dad quickly washes the dishes then goes down to set things up for this afternoon and I don't want to disturb him. After lunch I go through the house and put things away. Usually Dad keeps the house clean and tidy but he's been working all hours and the housework hasn't been done. I think about taking out the vacuum cleaner but it's really noisy.

At three o'clock, the downstairs doorbell rings. Dad has a separate door down there so his clients don't walk through the house. I hear raised voices so I peek downstairs to see Miranda Nessman with a man who I figured must be Bill. She says something about this being an expensive waste of time. Bill tells her that since this website is her idea she better be willing to do it right and doing it right means doing a proper focus group. I go back upstairs without disturbing them.

I am looking around for something to do when Dad comes upstairs. "Sorry, you heard that."

"Why is she being that way?" I frown.

"She thinks she knows exactly how the website should look. Bill insists on a proper job. Like kids on the playground they are fighting over who gets to decide what game to play." Dad sighs. "I need you to be diplomatic about it."

"What's that mean?"

"Pretend you did not hear and say nothing about it." Dad answers. "Miranda usually deals with the paperwork. Bill wants her to learn something about handling the creative side."

"Okay." I agree.

Dad glances around at the room. "Penny and the girls are likely to come to the front door, could you stay up here and answer it? Bring them downstairs when they get here." I nod. "And check out the window to see who it is before you open it."

"I won't let anyone else in." I promise.

"That better not be a tuna sandwich type promise." Dad warns.

"It won't be." I smile at him. I go into the living room to sit on the couch where I can see people coming to the front door. The loud voices stop a few minutes before a beat up van stops. Hailey is the first one out the passenger door. Six of the other girls get out the side door. Miss Penny finally gets out the driver's door. I go to the door and open it before they can even ring the bell.

"Hi." I call. "Come in."

Hailey reaches the door as I say it. She steps inside and stops in the entryway. "This is a nice house."

"Dad fixed it up after he bought it." I answer. "He even put in the flower garden."

The other girls gather until Miss Penny enters. I notice that Serena has not come. "Dad said to bring you downstairs to his office." I lead the way after making certain the front door is shut and locked again.

Chairs are put out in a semi-circle, on each chair seat is a box. "Come in, pick up the toys and sit down. Mr. Nessman will explain the toys before we start talking about your ideas. You too, Abby," I pick up the box and sit in the last chair. Hailey sits next to me.

Penny waits standing up at the back of the room until Dad moves his chair so she can sit behind us. She thanks him quietly and turns her attention to Bill.

"If you will each open the box," Bill starts as Miranda, who was sitting off to the side, pretends to be interested in her fingernails as the girls open the packages. "Inside you will find New Mark Toys computerized doll. Each doll is unique in many respects. These dolls are orphaned babies, babies who have a distinct ethnic background. They need to be feed, carried and rocked to sleep. Also included is a booklet that tells you the doll's name, something about how its parents or grandparents would have tended it and why it was placed for adoption."

"So it's a cross between a Cabbage Patch kid and a virtual pet?" Penny asks.

"A variation," Bill agrees. "The babies need kind, caring adoptive parents who will take the time to learn a little about how to make these babies comfortable if you would take the time to read the information about your doll."

I open my booklet and read about how my baby, whose name was in unreadable letters. The paper says my doll comes from a small tribe in Africa. "Can we rename our babies?" I ask.

"You could, but it would remove part of his or her heritage." Bill frowns.

"But if he's living with me and his name is hard to say then everyone will nickname him. If I give him a simpler name it will make things easier and he won't get teased as much. How do real parents who adopt kids from other countries do it?" I ask.

Bill frown, Dad shrugs, Penny hesitates then speaks. "I know a man who was adopted from Haiti. His parents gave him a new first name and used his old name for a middle name."

"I'm not sure this name would even translate to go on a birth certificate." I sigh.

Dad comes over and looks at the name. "I have no clue." He assures me.

Bill comes over. He glances at the name and says it. "Not everyone's a sociologist and a linguist." Miranda speaks for the first time. "Babies adapt, he should be able to learn to answer to a new name. Adoptive parents could be jailed if they treated their kids how some children in third world countries live."

"How would we know?" Hailey asks then pauses. "Could there be information on the website about different cultures and how they treat their babies compared to where we live."

Dad goes over to his desk and writes something down. Bill nods. "I have the information on a data base I use to program the dolls."

"What about on naming babies?" Rachel asks. "Can there be a list of names with meanings so we can find one that matches in meaning of the old name or one that somehow fits with both cultures."

Dad makes another note.

Bill waits for Dad to finish. "Once the computer program in the dolls are activated you have to immediately start looking after them, making certain they are feed and have clean clothes. They will sleep for ten to sixteen hours a day and once you find the way they like to be rocked to sleep you can wake them and get them to sleep to match a schedule. They will thrive if they are looked after properly but they get sick and shut themselves off if they are neglected. I don't suggest you all start them now but maybe one of you can and show the others."

"I will." Rachel volunteers. "I've had puppies so I know something about looking after babies."

"Alright, the way to activate the doll is to pick them up in your arms and hug them tight around the middle." Bill instructs. Rachel follows his directions. "Okay, now if you look at the read out display on the doll's stomach. It will tell you what you have to do to look after him or her."

Rachel lifts the doll's top. "Hold her up so everyone can see. This display shows if the doll needs to be feed, if she needs a change of clothes and whether the doll is sick or healthy. To feed the doll there is a bottle, changing the doll requires the use of a reusable wipe, sickness is treated with attention and a medicine bottle, all included in the box."

"How does the doll know if it's had attention?" Carly, usually the quiet one in Sunday school, asks.

"There are sensors built into the skin. If the doll is handled too little it gets sick and if it's handled too much it gets sick. That's also how it knows if it's been changed or feed."

"You shouldn't call the baby it the book says whether the doll is a he or she."

Hailey objects.

Dad makes another note.

"Picture of how to feed, change and treat the baby when she gets sick would be good." Rachel speaks up. "Can there be a place for girls to give hints and tips to other adoptive mothers about getting the baby on a schedule."

Dad keeps writing. Bill takes a deep breath. "Okay, Rachel is your baby a he or a she."

"She's a girl." Rachel looks in her book. "Ingrid."

Bill glances at the dark skinned baby. "Ingrid? That baby isn't Swedish."

"No, but she looks like the woman from Casablanca to me." Rachel shrugs. "I can't read her real name."

Miranda hoots. We all stare at her but she just breaks out in giggles. The sound of it makes me want to giggle too but I know how serious Dad takes his focus group. Rachel gets upset. "The baby has the same shaped face."

Miranda tries to calm down but she can't seem to stop giggling. "It's not you I find funny, honey." She manages in spite of the laughter. "It's Bill." The last word spills out of her.

"It's not his fault he doesn't think like a girl." Rachel thinks about what she said then a tiny giggle escapes her. I glance at Dad and he winks at me. I can't help it but start giggling too. The other girls join in.

Bill throws up his hands and his glance roams from Dad to Penny.

"Girls, Mr. Hansen needs our ideas." Penny tries to stay serious but I can tell by the look in her eye she is giggling inside.

We try to get serious but every time we look at Miranda or each other we start to giggle again. Dad let us go on for about a while then he stands up.

"Girls, I need your help with a few other things. Like what colours do I make the backgrounds for the pages?" Suddenly we become serious again.

Carly clears her throat. "The box is pretty. Can't you use those colours?"

I take another look at the box, Carly is right it is pretty. "It's nice and multi-coloured." I say. "So you'd have lots of choices for combinations."

Dad picks up the box from my doll and studies it. "Anyone have any other ideas?"

"I vote you keep the pattern and vary the colours." Hailey says. "I like the way the wavy parts flow together."

"I like the idea it gives the site product tie in." Miranda smiles at us.

Bill shrugs. "Packaging is Miranda's department."

"Okay." Dad agrees. "Now I need a name for the site. This is very important but there are rules everyone has to understand about making suggestions. The Internet is a very big place and certain words can send little girls to sites that are only for adults. I don't want to use the words: doll, baby, or girls. So I would like you to each take a paper and pencil. Write down your suggestions and I will go over them. We need something that a young girl would associate with computerized babies but nothing that would trigger adult sites." He hands paper and pencils around the group. He hands them to Bill and Miranda too. "I would like as many suggestions as you can give me but I do not promise to use any of them."

We work quietly for a long time. My list isn't very long but I notice Hailey has quite a few. I hope she has come up with something good.

Dad comes over to me. "Abby, can you go get a stack of small plates, spoons and the ice-cream scoop?"

"Sure." I hand him my list.

Miss Penny stands up. "I will get them."

"Abby knows where they are." Dad objects.

"Then I will help her carry them." Miss Penny offers and comes upstairs with me. I open the cupboard where the plates are. Penny lifts them down then closes the cupboard. I open the drawer and take out spoons and the scoop out of the drawer then open another drawer for paper napkins. We go back downstairs and Dad motions to his desk so we place everything there.

"If you could hand me your lists," Dad interrupts everyone. The downstairs doorbell rings. Dad nods to Bill, who goes to the door. The girls hand in their lists.

"We want to thank you for your help." Bill comes back with three pizza boxes and a grocery bag. He sets them on the desk and opens the first box. It is a dessert pizza with strawberry sauce, slices of strawberries, icing and chocolate. The second is apple, nuts, icing and chocolate. And the third was blueberries and raspberries on a strawberry sauce with icing and chocolate. The ice cream is in a pail in the bag.

Everyone has a small piece of each pizza with a scoop of ice-cream, even Miranda, who seems happier after her fit of giggles. After we are finished eating, Dad has everyone stack used plates on the corner of the desk.

Bill clears his throat. "Girls, this has been a very enlightening afternoon. To reward you for your part in it I am giving you the dolls you opened. I hope you will enjoy them."

"Now, I promised to get the girls home by five so we have to go." Miss Penny glances at her watch.

Most of the girls pick up their dolls and follow Miss Penny to the downstairs entrance. Hailey comes over to me. "You have the best dad."

"Hailey," Miss Penny calls.

"I'll call you." Hailey promises and runs to catch up with the rest of the girls.

I pick up my doll and her box. "Abby, I have to talk with Bill and Miranda for a few minutes so go up and I will be up to make supper in a while."

"I'm not hungry." I say Dad laughs as I walk up the stairs. To tell the truth the thought the idea of kd after all that dessert was kind of sickening.

CHAPTER 5

I go up to my room and do another chapter of my novel study including the questions. I am finished and staring at my math book when Dad calls.

I go downstairs. "I'm really not hungry."

"Good thing, supper is late. Hailey is on the phone." Dad answers.

I pick up the receiver. "Hello."

"Abby." Hailey sounds a little breathless. "What are you doing this week?"

"This week, homework," I admit. Dad frowns at me but I just shrug.

"I know, my mom's working so she and we can't do anything together either. It's just I don't have any sisters or brothers and I thought that maybe you could come along with me to computer camp."

"What?" I ask.

"Computer Camp; I wanted to sign up for it, but I don't know anyone else who's going and I'm kind of scared." Hailey admits. "I checked, with the teacher, there's room for more campers."

"I'd have to ask Dad and learn about what it costs." I don't want to wreck this friendship so I think maybe he'll turn her down for me.

"Miss Penny will talk to your dad about it." Hailey offers.

"Give me a minute." I hold the phone so that Hailey can't hear. "Dad, Hailey wants me to go to a computer camp with her. She says she's asked if there's room."

Dad gives me his thoughtful expression. I shrug. "She doesn't want to go alone. She says Miss Penny would give you the details."

"Get her to put Miss Penny on the phone."

"Hailey, he hasn't said yes or no but he's willing to talk to Miss Penny," I speak after putting the phone to my ear.

"Here she is," Hailey says. I hand the phone to Dad.

Dad takes the phone. "What is this about a computer camp?" He listens for a long time. "We are not talking overnight?" He listens again. "What does it cost?" I see that look, the one he gets when he's figuring out whether he can afford something. "Where is it?" He interrupts. "I can drive half the time?" Then he falls silent for a long time. "Okay, Abby will be ready to go by eight-thirty in the morning." He hands the phone back to me.

"Abby, it's wonderful." Hailey sounds excited.

"Wonderful." I try to act happy but computer camp! "What do I need to bring?"

"Just yourself and lunch just like going to school." Hailey answers. "It's school hours. We'll pick you up at your house."

"I'll be ready." I agree.

"Miss Penny says I have to go now," Hailey says. "See you tomorrow."

"Bye." I manage before she hangs up. I turn to Dad, "Computer Camp!"

Dad tries hard to keep from smiling but finally breaks out laughing. "Maybe they can teach you something new."

"Right!" I sigh, "Why did you even agree?"

"If you stay home, you will sit around all week worry yourself sick about that math." Dad shrugs. "You have used a computer the worst thing that can happen is you learn more about it than me."

I roll my eyes. Dad had given me my first lesson in computers before I was two, my second language is C. Actually it was his way of keeping me entertained while he finished his degree in computer science. I sigh and go back to my room, another change and all because I couldn't answer one math question.

I look in my textbook one more time before I go to bed. I sigh, I try to think of ways of avoiding trouble with math. Somehow without going back to Friday afternoon nothing comes to mind. I think about computer camp and how I can stay out of trouble there but I lack any real information about what happens there. I fall asleep fretting. The same dream only, this time, the man at the door keeps changing, one second my grandfather is there, then Mr. Richter takes his place, then they flip places again. I must not have screamed this time because Dad does not come. It takes me a long time to go back to sleep.

Dad packs my lunch while I eat breakfast the next morning. It's not like I couldn't have made my own cheese sandwich but Dad has funny ideas about being a parent. Mrs. Martins insists that Serena does housework.

My dad never insists that I do anything.

"Where's your backpack?"

"Up in my room, I'll get it." I volunteer, putting down my fork.

"Once you are done your breakfast."

I finish my pancakes then I go upstairs for my backpack. I put my lunch into it and Dad hands me a cheque. "Give that to the person in charge."

"Okay." I tuck it in a pocket. "What time are you expecting me?"

"Before supper, about the same time, you would get home from school."

I nod.

"Have fun and keep busy." Dad gives me a hug.

The front doorbell rings. I go to answer it. Hailey stands on the steps. "Come on."

I follow her out to the van where Miss Penny waits. "Hello." I greet her.

"Climb in." Miss Penny instructs.

"Why are you driving us?" I ask after I sit in the back seat of the van.

"Because I work at the recreation centre where the camp is being held," Miss Penny answers. "Are you all buckled up?"

I do up my seat belt and sit back. It is only a five-minute drive to the center. Hailey seems very familiar with the place. She drags me away from Miss Penny the instant we get there. Hailey leads me down three or four halls and into a room full of computer desks.

"Randy, this is Abby. She's the girl I phoned about." Hailey speaks to a man not much older than Dad.

"Hi Abby, we have to get you registered."

"Dad gave me a cheque to cover the fees." I pull the paper from my pocket.

"Okay, then we will take you down to the office before class starts." Randy nods toward a woman who nods back. "Come with me."

I follow Randy back down the hall and into an office. The lady behind the desk takes my name and Dad's cheque. She also gives me a bunch of forms for Dad to fill out and a receipt before we go back to the class.

Randy clears his throat. "This isn't the beginner's class but I also teach beginners so if you get stuck just wave me over."

"My Dad taught me some stuff about computers." I admit.

"Okay, just take a seat by Hailey and we'll get started." Randy smiles at me.

I sit down at the computer next to Hailey. The woman stands at the front of the room, "If everyone would turn on their computers."

I search the machine until I find the switch. Hailey watches me then starts her own computer. "We will be learning word processing today using Word from Office 2000."

The screen comes up and I choose the desktop icon for Word and double click on it. Hailey follows. "Does everyone have Word up on the desktop?" The woman asks. Randy comes to glance at the computers.

He nods at me. The woman starts again. "We are going to learn how to set the size and style of the letters. We begin by clicking the Format tab at the top of the page. Then we click on font."

I open the font box and click around a bit. I choose wing dings in a large size. I close the box and write my name. Hailey looks over. "What's that?"

"Wingdings." I answer. I open the font box again, highlight the letters I change the font to French script.

My name changes into fancy writing complete with swirls. Then I change it again to Garamond and make it smaller so Hailey can read it. Then I highlight and bold it.

Hailey turns to her computer and opens the font box. She clicks on a font then tries typing. "Hailey, are you listening?" Randy asks.

Hailey reddens. "I was just copying Abby. She knows how to use fonts. She used three or four different ones and can make them bold."

Randy pauses. "Let's see what you can do, Abby."

"Do you want individual faces and sizes or complete styles?" I ask.

"Huh?" Randy asks, "Styles?"

"You can set up font styles in Word." I shrug. "Here I'll show you." I go to the Format tab and choose styles instead of fonts. I click on new and the next box opens I set the font style and type, the paragraph style and name it then I hit apply. I came back to the document choose that name from the font list and type using it.

"Where did you learn that?" Randy asks.

"My dad."

Randy pauses, "How about if you help Hailey this morning? We can talk about what programs you know at lunch. Okay?"

"Okay." I agree. After that, we ignore the teacher at the front of the room. I show Hailey how to set the page size, do borders, add drop caps, add backgrounds, colour the letters, choose a theme, set up tables of different kinds and use the grammar and spell checkers. Hailey thinks it is all so neat and we get so involved that Randy has to come over and tell us it is break time.

We go outside to a small field where we play a game of dodge ball until it is time to go back inside. We meet Miss Penny in the hall. "How are you doing?" She asks.

"Abby's a whiz at computers, she's shown me lots of stuff." Hailey answers.

"I hope you are not too bored." Miss Penny speaks to me.

"I would be but Hailey's excitement is catchy. It's fun watching her learn." I answer truthfully.

Miss Penny smiles, "I hope the rest of the day goes as well."

I smile back at her but Hailey is already dragging me back to the computer room.

This time, Randy stands at the front of the room. "What we are going to do now is design an invitation for your parents and our sponsors to come Friday afternoon. By then we hope to produce some work to show them how far you've come with your computer skills. We will have some refreshments and each student will show at least one piece of work."

Hailey's hand shoots up. "Can we make it fancy?"

"We might be able to but first we have to get the right information on it." Randy explains. "Fancy doesn't get you far if no one knows where we are or why we want them to come. Let's start with the relevant information. What do we need to put on the invitation?"

A bigger boy in front speaks up without raising his hand. "The Gladwin Recreation Centre's Advanced Computer Camp would like to invite you to come to its end of camp showing. That's how it started last year."

"We could say that or we might want to change it. How do the people who weren't here last year feel?"

I put up my hand, "That kind of work are we showing?" I want to know what I should expect.

"That depends on the skill level of the person, some people make websites, others write and print poetry or short stories, and someone else might use this time to do research and set up a display for a science fair project with tables or a power point presentation." Randy answers. "It depends on your interest. Later today we will discuss with each of you what programs we have and which ones you want to learn. We would prefer if whatever you choose to do it be with a program you learn this week."

"Does anyone have any other suggestions for an opening line?" Randy asks.

A girl to my left puts up her hand. "Does everyone have to do something or could we do group projects?"

Randy sighs and glances at the other teacher. "Group projects need our approval. We would need to know that everyone in the group put effort into learning something and did part of the work. It would need to be a bigger project that just one person could do." The woman answers.

"How big?" The girl asks.

"Website with multiple pages or ten pages of poetry made into a book or a complicated presentation of some kind," She answers. "Like I said the idea would need pre-approval."

Hailey whispers. "Let's do something together."

I bite my lip I have no idea what programs they had or what we can do. "What would we do?" I ask.

"A website?" Hailey whispers back.

"It's got to be with a program I've never used before." I whisper and glance at the icons on the screen. They were all too familiar. I click start then programs and shake my head.

Hailey sighs. "Maybe they have different programs from what your dad has."

"Only if it's on a different computer," I answer.

"There's got to be something you haven't done."

Hailey starts to be interrupted by Randy, "Hailey and Abby!"

"We were talking about what to do." I answer.

"That's a discussion for later this afternoon, right now we have to draft the invitation." Randy states. "Now give me an opening line."

Hailey smiles, "How about The Gladwin Recreation Center presents: Computer Camp Masterpieces?"

"That's good." The older boy jeers, "If you can produce a masterpiece."

Hailey blushes. Randy steps in. "That is enough! That kind of talk is unacceptable! Give us something better rather than tearing down someone else's ideas."

The boy smirks but says nothing else. A girl to my right raises her hand. "What if we used projects instead of masterpieces?"

"Masterpieces sound more exciting." The girl to my left objects. "Like an advertisement."

"Are we advertising or creating an invitation?" Randy asks.

"We want people to come, don't we?" A boy right in the front asks.

"How about Parents, Sponsors and Computer Geeks; the Gladwin Recreational Center presents Visions from Geekdom's Young Minds?" The nasty older boy asks.

I sigh. Hailey raises her hand. "There is no such word as Geekdom."

Randy pauses. "This is getting out of hand, we know that it's the Gladwin Recreation Centre; Friday March the 23rd at three P.M. and we're inviting parents and sponsors. I'm going to give you each a chance to design an invitation. We'll vote on which invitation gets sent."

I put up my hand. "Why can't we each just design one to take home?"

"That would be good for parents and you could each take your own home but we need some invitations for sponsors so we'll choose one or two to make more than one copy." Randy answers. "Use Word since that's what you learned about this morning."

I open a new document. I think for a long time then remember an invitation Dad received once to an artist's showing in a gallery. I copy the style, and size.

The Gladwin Recreational Centre invites you to a showing of student work

On Friday March 23 at 3:00 P.M.

Refreshments will be served.

I look at it for a long time but somehow it lacks something. I add a nice marbled background like the gallery invitation but I still not happy with it. Dad won't care I will be the one to put it in his calendar.

Randy comes to look over my shoulder. "That looks nice, very classy."

I shake my head. "I don't like it." I highlight everything and am going to hit the delete button but Randy stops me.

"What's wrong with it?" He asks.

I look at it for a long time. "It's too- I don't know- it just is."

"How about if you used something other than straight lines or add a more modern font?" He asks. "You know how to change fonts."

I go to the font box and change it to Dakota, and then I arch the first line. Then I go up to themes and choose a more colourful one. I stare at it for a long time.

"Do you like that better?" Randy asks.

I couldn't tell him that the invitation isn't important to me, so I just nod.

"Save it to the campers work file then you can print it

out so we can compare it to the rest of the invitations. The colour printer is not the default but the second one on the list." Randy tells me.

I send the invitation to the printer. Then turn my mind to the problem of what program to use to create a web site, it will have to be a site and not just a page if it was a group project. I go through the available programs again. I sigh.

"Abby, look at my invitation," Hailey calls to me.

I glance over but it is hard to read she used letters in every size shape and colour all mixed together, words go in every direction and I have to look very hard to recognize words. "Well that do you think?" She asks.

"It's colourful." I latch on to my father's trick of not really giving an option. He does what when he doesn't want to hurt my feelings.

"I wonder if it will be picked." Her eyes light up.

"I don't know." I lie. "It depends on who gets to choose."

"Where's yours?"

"I sent it to the printer. Randy said to use the colour printer which isn't the default but the next one on the list."

"What does default mean?" Hailey's forehead wrinkles.

"The default is the printer the computer would use if you didn't tell it to use another one." I try to explain but I am not sure she understands.

"Can you show me?" Hailey asks.

"Click on file. Choose print from the drop list. Click the arrow on the end. Choose the second printer on the list. Now tell the computer to print by clicking OK." I give the directions as she moves through the process.

"Why would they have more than one printer?" Hailey

asks.

"Because the first one only prints in black and white which is what they want people to use most of the time, colour costs more to print per page." I explain.

"Oh!" Hailey frowns. "How come you know so much?"

"Dad told me," Which is the answer to everything I know about computers.

Randy comes over. "Hailey, is your invitation finished?"

"Abby just helped me print it." Hailey answers.

"Did you save it to the campers work file?" Randy asks.

"No." Hailey shakes her head.

"Well save it then we'll look over the invitations people made." Randy answers before walking away.

I start to turn back to my computer when Hailey asks. "Please, help me."

"Go to file." I watch as she does it. "Click on save as." The box comes up. "Okay, name it Hailey's invitation." She types it in, having to stop and correct twice. "Click on campers work." She does that. "Now click on save." She does and the box disappears.

"Did it go to the right place?" Hailey whispers.

"Go file." I instruct. "Click on open." The box opens up. "Click on campers work." She does so. "Look for Hailey's invitation."

"There it is." She takes a deep breath.

"Okay, you can either click on it to bring it up or you can close the box."

Randy stands at the front of the class and clears his voice. "We have everyone's invitations. I've laid them out on the table at the side. Everyone will walk past them and choose the one they like best and vote by putting a check mark on a paper below each invitation. The first row will start."

I go with my row. I vote for a funny invitation where someone has included clip art. I wince when I see that my invitation had a few votes but Hailey's has none. I sit down. Hailey's row goes next headed by the boy who has been nasty earlier.

"Look at this one, you can't read a word." He announces in a loud voice holding up Hailey's invitation. Hailey blushes and looks down.

"Travis, I've warned you once, we do not make negative comments in this class." Randy answers. "You are not to move or show any work other than your own. Another incident and you will be asked to leave."

Travis puts the paper down but the damage has been done. I'm not certain Hailey voted for anyone. She comes back to the desk sniffling back tears. "Why didn't you tell me it was bad?" She whispers then turns away.

After the last camper files past, Randy walks past the table he picks mine out of the whole works. "This invitation got the most votes. We'll print more of this one to send to our sponsors, the rest you can take the one you made home to your parents."

I frown. I suppose I should be happy but I feel like I have let down Hailey both by not telling her the truth, and then by having mine chosen. "We'll take our lunch break."

CHAPTER 6

I reach for my backpack but Hailey gets up and leaves the room. I sit looking at my lunch in silence. Randy comes over. "Abby, have you looked at the programs on the computer?"

I nod.

"Is there anything you haven't used before?" He asks.

"No." I rearrange my cheese sandwich but don't take a bite. "Dad uses all these and a few more."

"What exactly have you done?" He asks.

"Mostly I watched while Dad worked. I got tired and he said I should try reading or watching movies instead."

"What does your Dad do?"

"He creates websites mostly, although he did a computer game once."

"I like computer games. What was his like?" He asks.

"Does this computer have internet access?" I ask.

"Yes, but the rules for using it are pretty strict." Randy frowns.

"Is it okay if you're right here?"

"Yeah," He nods.

I go to Dad's favourite games site and choose the game we worked on together. "Try playing it." I stand up and offer him my chair.

Randy clicks on play and is off shooting around the galaxy playing intergalactic tourist. You collect unusual pets and sometimes have to fight off exotic diseases all while dodging the locals who think your spaceship is a UFO and you a dangerous invader. Randy gets caught on the second planet and they vaporize him.

"That's different." Randy comments.

"That's Dad, he only does original stuff." I shrug.

"So, what did you help with?" Randy asks.

"I helped storyboard, I thought up some of the animals and that sort of thing. Dad did the artwork." I acknowledge.

"The other campers liked your invitation."

"It wasn't very original. I copied the design from a gallery invitation."

"Then you changed it which made it your own. Not everything has to be entirely original to be good."

I shrug. I am more concerned with where Hailey went. I feel sick for not telling her the truth while she had time to change her invitation.

"We have one computer with an older version of Flash. You could do a short game where you did the artwork yourself." Randy suggests.

I pause. "Hailey wanted me to do something with her."

"Hailey needs to start smaller. It would be better if she did something on her own." Randy says. The way he said it made me realize that even if Hailey still wanted to, they weren't going to let us work together. "Come with me, I'll move you to the Flash computer."

I have little choice but to pack up my stuff. I hope at least to talk to Hailey rather than her just coming back and finding me gone. Randy walks to the front of the class.

"Travis, I'm going to have to get you to move."

The boy looks startled. "I sat here first."

"I know, but Abby needs the computer with Flash on it for her project." Randy answers. "You can learn photo editing where she was sitting."

My heart shudders. Hailey will have to sit beside Travis. "Can we just move the computers?" I speak softly but the two of them just glare at each other and make no sign of having heard me.

"You told me I wasn't to sit at the back last camp."

"Hopefully, you've matured somewhat since last year." Randy answers. "Now I'm telling you to move."

Travis shoots me an angry glance like the whole thing is my fault. He gathers his stuff and moves to the back of the room. I don't want to take the spot but Randy instructs me to "Sit and finish my lunch."

I take a bite, but the bread and cheese sticks to the top of my mouth. I sip my juice until I manage to swallow that bite. After eating half of it, I wrap it back up. I stand. The woman teacher is sitting at a table so I go over. "Excuse me, but could you please tell me where the bathrooms are?"

"Down the hall, on your right," Her tone is brisk and efficient but she doesn't look up. I follow her directions until I find the door marked Ladies room. It is empty I go to the bathroom and wash my hands and wish I'd never heard of computer camp.

Hailey doesn't come back until I have to be back at my desk, I hear her voice behind me and I glance around. She doesn't look my way. Not that I have much time to spend looking around the room.

Dad had taken nearly a year working on Tourists from Outer Space to finish ten planets. It had taken weeks just to complete details on the original concept. I have to create a game all by myself and finish it by Friday. I think about all the steps we had done and tried to figure out shortcuts. I know I can't draw it myself, no matter what Randy says, I don't have time.

My mind goes blank. I wish I am visiting and learning about the dinosaurs instead. Dinosaurs! How about dinosaurs? Fighting dinosaurs but I realize that would take too much time making them move and interact. Matching dinosaurs but I realize I won't need Flash for that. Identifying dinosaurs from behind plants and trees, the dinosaur won't have to move but the trees will so that you can see if you guessed right nor not. I can scan pictures and cut them from their background then mix them together.

I own at least three books at home about dinosaurs. I can pick out my favourites. I finally manage to take a deep breath I have an idea.

I put up my hand. "Yes, Abby." Randy answers.

"Could I have some paper and a pencil to write out my story?" I ask.

Randy seems startled, but Dad always starts with a paper plan and it doesn't matter whether it is a game or a website. "I suppose." He finally manages. "I'll have to go find some." He leaves the room and comes back some time later. "Does anyone else want paper for writing or planning?" He asks.

I have the paper. Now I need someone walking in the trees trying to identify dinosaurs. I consider a man coming off a space ship or a time machine. It sounded too much like Outer Space Tourist. A caveman, no, scientists didn't think man and dinosaurs lived at the same time. Who lived at the same time as dinosaurs? The only answer I could come up with was other dinosaurs. What kind of dinosaur would be trying to guess other types of dinosaurs; a small dinosaur looking not to get eaten? People don't like games that were too hard to win that's why Outer Space Tourist never sold, or that's what Dad says; a predator looking for prey; people don't like to think of themselves as bloodthirsty. When else did dinosaurs look for each other?

It takes me a long time but I work out an answer. Parents looked for lost children. I can have a T-Rex looking for his baby. I start to write. Baby T-Rex is lost and his Daddy is looking for Baby T-Rex. He has to look behind all the plants and trees. First, he will hear the dinosaurs then he will move closer until they come into full sight. You have three chances to identify the dinosaur, you will get three points for just the sound, two points for the sound and seeing one part of the dinosaur, one point for the sound and most of the dinosaur, and no points for guesses after seeing the whole dinosaur. Afterward, the dinosaurs will flee from T-Rex and he will have to start again until he finds his child. Winning the game will depend on getting enough points to find the Baby T-Rex.

I still am not sure how to make the last part happen but I am supposed to learn something so I leave it like that. First I have to find sounds dinosaurs made.

"Abby, if you have your ideas together, you need to open the program and start learning to use it." Randy comes up behind me.

"Can I go on the internet to do research?"

"We have to send forms home and get your parents

to sign them before you have permission to use the Internet." Randy shakes his head. "You need to open the program."

So I open Flash and made balls bounce and things crash but it is a waste of time. I need to get the contents of the game together before Flash is going to do me any good. I sigh.

Then an idea strikes me and I look in the Flash sound library but except for a few everyday sounds its empty. Dinosaurs died a long time ago, who knows what noises they made. I open the first sound then go into the editor and try to stretch it out, make it deeper or higher, or change it to short bursts of sound. I save an edited sound to the library then open another sound and change it. I save that one.

I feel eyes on me, I look up the woman instructor, her eyes are all shiny and her mouth is all puckered up. "Is it really necessary to make all that noise?"

"Sorry." I mutter. Randy goes over to talk to her but I know I have to come up with another source of sounds. I'll have to look on the Internet at home if Dad isn't using both of his computers.

I go back to the screen; I split the screen with bands of colour, light blue on top, green in the middle and brown on the bottom. I try to make objects put in the center of the screen look like they are moving to the sides as if I am getting closer to them so they are getting further apart.

Randy appears by my side. "Those were pretty scary sounds, what were they?"

"I was trying to make sounds of different kinds of dinosaurs." I shrug. "I'll have to search the Internet at home."

"No. All work on the projects must be done here. Other kids don't have a computer at home and it's not fair to them. Besides, we want the project to reflect what you did here."

"She doesn't like me making noise." I frown.

"Sound editing has been part of many projects campers have worked on. MaryAnn has a headache today and probably should have stayed home. By the middle of the week, there will be other kids working with sound and music, and once you get your parents' permission to go on the Internet, you can research from here." Randy tries to reassure me. I don't suppose I look convinced. "You have all week." Randy turns and walks away.

I go back to moving objects around to see if I can get the walking into the screen look. How fast would T-Rex walk? I try moving two trees out from the middle of the screen at different speeds. Then I realize to make it look right I have to have a background of trees. I spend a long time trying to draw individual trees then gave up and made lollipop looking trees, two straight lines with a round shape on top.

When Randy calls the break in the afternoon, I try to move close enough to apologize to Hailey but they break us into two teams to play hide and seek. Then I really can't get near her, as she and her teammates scramble to move to a new hiding spot if I get close.

We return to class. I turn on my computer and look in the campers work file for my file but it isn't there. I put up my hand. Randy comes over. "What's wrong?"

"My file is gone." I frown. "The one I was working on before the break."

"You're sure you saved it properly?" Randy asks.

I nod. "I saved it."

"What did you save it as?"

"Abby dash project," I say then add. "No spaces between."

"I'll check." Randy goes to the computer on the front desk He spends maybe five minutes looking at things then comes back. "Sorry Abby, it got deleted by mistake."

I take a deep breath. I have to remember to bring a disk so it can't happen again. I start over to create the backdrop and the trees. I get back to where I was before minus my stored sounds and Randy announces it is time to go home. I save the file again then check that it is in the campers work file.

I grab my backpack and look around for Hailey. She is gone. I start for the door then try to remember the way to the parking lot. I start out to the right but realize I have made a mistake when I get to the first bend in the hallway. I turned around and go back walking slowly until think I recognize something then follow that hallway. I get to the end of it and don't recognize anything. A fluttering sensation starts in my chest. I turn and go back the way I came. I take a deep breath and then another deep breath. Then I see the computer room door. I know where I am but I don't know which way to go. I stop in the hall.

"It is bad enough you flirt with Penny. Now you are going out of your way for Hailey and her new friend."

"May I remind you knowing Penny gets us these jobs, and without Hailey's new friend this camp would be kaput. The rent doesn't pay itself."

"I could have got us a job through Rob."

I let out a little sob.

Randy steps out of the room. "Abby, what's wrong?"

"I can't find the parking lot." My voice sounds strange.

"You came with Hailey, didn't you?" He asks and I nod. "Come on, I'll show you."

"Randy, we've got to clean up this mess." MaryAnn

demands his attention inside the room.

"I'll be back as soon as I make certain Abby gets safely to Penny." Randy answers. "Why don't you take your headache home? I'll finish up here."

There is no answer but I sense her disapproval. Randy points back down the way I'd just come but half way down he opens a door and steps into a side hall. I follow but I stay three steps behind him.

We meet Penny coming in to find me. "There you are. I told Hailey she should have waited for you."

"Sorry, but I couldn't find my way out. Randy was showing me the way."

"Thank you." Penny says to Randy but she doesn't smile at him. "Come on, we better get you home before your Dad decides I am irresponsible." She holds out her hand.

I hesitate before taking it, I sometimes hold Dad's hand especially in a crowd but I don't usually touch other people. I turn. "Bye, Randy."

"See you tomorrow, Abby." He winks at me. I don't know what to say so I turn and walk with Miss Penny.

"Is something wrong?" Penny asks just before we step outside.

"He winked at me." It is the first thing out of my mouth even though I am still worried about Hailey thinking I'd betrayed her.

Penny laughs, but it comes out more as a ladylike snort. "Randy winks at lots of females. Pay no attention."

We go to her van. I get in the back seat and do up my seatbelt. I think about apologizing to Hailey right there, but I don't want to do it in front of Miss Penny and embarrass Hailey with an explanation. Hailey doesn't say anything to me, not that she lifts her nose in the air the way Serena does; instead, she seems extremely interested in the toe of her sneaker. My stomach still feels a little sick.

"How did the day go?" Miss Penny asks.

I think this may be a chance to explain to Hailey. "Randy moved me to a computer with Flash on it."

"What's Flash?" Miss Penny asks.

"It's an animation program for making cartoons and moving pictures." I bite my lip. "He suggested I make a computer game."

"Wow!" Miss Penny answers. "That sounds exciting."

"It's too much work," I answer. "I can't finish it by Friday."

"You will, you're a whiz," Hailey breaks into the conversation. "Since I'm just a beginner I have to start small. Randy suggested I desktop publish one of my poems in Word."

"You've got lots of them to choose from." Penny answers.

"I wanted to do something more exciting." Hailey frowns. "Like a web page."

Miss Penny doesn't answer her as we get to my house and she pulls over to the curb. "We'll pick you up again tomorrow at eight-thirty."

I undo my seatbelt. "Thank you for the ride." I glance at Hailey, but she still will not look at me. I open the door and get out. Miss Penny waits until I go into the house before she pulls away. I drop my backpack on a chair and go downstairs. Dad works at the computer. I go over for a hug.

"Hi." I say.

"Abby." He glances at his watch. "You are home late."

"I got lost looking for the parking lot." I grimace.

"I will be up in a little while to make supper." Dad kisses my cheek and directs me back toward the stairs with one hand. "I've got to finish this section of programming before I dare take a break."

I go up to the kitchen and open my backpack to take the uneaten portion out of my sandwich and put it in the garbage before Dad sees it. I find the papers Dad needs to fill out. I put them at his place at the table. Then I take my backpack upstairs.

I pick up my novel study book and read another chapter I am just looking at the questions when Dad calls me downstairs.

"What's this?"

"Registration forms for the camp." I answer when I can see what he is talking about.

"I understand those but this one is on Internet access?" Dad is frowning.

"We have to do a project and if it involves research, then we have to get our parent's permission to go on the Internet." I explain.

"No Internet, unless I can supervise you," Dad places the form to one side. "You will have to do your research at home or find another project."

"But I can't do it at home I can only work at camp because they want to prove they taught me something." I protest softly.

"Sorry, Abby-girl but no." Dad uses his firm voice and I know he won't change his mind.

"Okay, no Internet." I agree but by the time I reach my room I know my game is doomed. I will not get it finished and Travis will show everyone and laugh. My cheeks get warm at the prospect of that happening in front of Hailey, Miss Penny and the other parents. If I hadn't messed up that math class, I'd be visiting dinosaurs instead of embarrassing myself in a computer class.

Rosalyn Marie Francis

CHAPTER 7

Miss Penny, rather than Hailey, comes to the door the next morning. She smiles at me but it isn't her full smile. "You ready to go?"

With my lunch in my backpack and an achy feeling in my stomach, I nod. We get in the van. Hailey is still studying the toe of her shoe. I don't try to talk to her I just buckle up and wait until we get to the recreational centre. I match Hailey's speed in getting out of the car and into the building. "Hailey, can I talk to you for a minute?"

Hailey takes a deep breath before stopping. "What?"

"I want to apologize for not saying that your invitation was hard to read. I really felt terrible when Travis held it up." I try to get the words to come out right but Hailey's cheeks coloured and I know that I'd embarrassed her again. "I just wanted to say I'm sorry." I sigh.

Hailey turns and walks toward the computer room. I follow behind walking slowly memorizing the way wishing she would say something so I know if she is still mad at me.

Randy stands at the door greeting the campers. MaryAnn sits at the computer on the table. I stop and hand my papers to Randy. "Dad said no Internet." I tell him then go sit at the computer with Flash on it.

I turn on the computer then opened the file. My file was missing again. I put up my hand.

MaryAnn comes over. "What is it?"

"My file has been deleted."

"You probably didn't save it right." She remarks.

"I checked to see that it had been saved." I answer. "It was here when I left last night."

"Well, you'll just have to start again." She turns around and walks away.

I pause then look for my invitation, it is gone too. I pause and look at the files that are left. Hailey's is missing and I frown. Hailey probably doesn't know how to delete it but she doesn't want more attention paid to it so I keep silent.

I open Flash and start again. I skip the green band of colour and just make the bottom part brown and the top part blue. I draw lollipop trees again and duplicate them. This time, I put everything on guidelines so they automatically move closer and to the right or left. I add a fern, which I duplicate and mix with the trees only I put them close together when they move to the front of the screen. I play with what I have made but it is wrong. The trees do not get bigger as they get closer to the front of the screen.

I put up my hand. Randy comes over. "What's wrong?"

"My trees need to get bigger as they get closer to the front of the screen." I frown. "How do I get them to do that?"

"Try drawing two trees different sizes and tween them." Randy suggests, "It's just like making a ball bounce but it changes the shape in this case makes them bigger."

I sigh but before I can ask him another question Randy is off to help someone else. I realize I can use this program but I can't do use it well enough to do anything as complicated as a computer game.

I glance back at Hailey, who looks nothing like her usual excited self. I see Travis's lips moving and know he is keeping up a running commentary that no one else can hear. I turn back around.

"Okay everyone, break time." Randy announces.

I slip a disk from my backpack and into the computer. "Abby? John? "

"I'm just saving my work." I answer, which is the truth I save it once to the camper's file and once to my disk. Randy makes impatient noises so I leave the disk in the computer and join the line of kids going outside.

Hailey smiles, "Thanks." We play dodge ball. I stay to the outside and last almost to the end. Travis targets Hailey early. I go to stand beside her after I get hit. I don't say anything I just stand there watching the end of the game.

I go back inside and find my file wasn't on the camper's work but I have another copy on my disk. I start right away to find some way to make the trees and ferns bigger. I go through every drop file looking for a tool to help me. I am starting on the second drop tab when I heard a sob.

I turn to see a tear slide down Hailey's face. "I know I saved it." Travis mocks her silently behind Randy's back. "I always check to make sure it's there, just like Abby told me too."

"Abby's been losing her own files." MaryAnn answers. "She's no one to teach you anything."

I bite my tongue. It isn't my conversation. "There have been a lot of files going missing." Randy frowns. "I'm going to check the computer records and if I find out who's doing it. They will be out of the camp."

Randy goes over to the computer on the desk and sits down. "You'll have to start over." MaryAnn tells Hailey and walks away. Hailey puts her hands over her face. Travis says something I see his lips move. Hailey gets up and flees the room.

I sigh before turning back to my project. I continue checking through the drop files. I am not even looking backwards when I hear a deep voice behind me. "Randy and MaryAnn, I'd like to see you in my office. Campers, Mrs. Wilson will stay and watch over you."

I turn my head to see the woman who had taken Dad's cheque step into the room. MaryAnn follows the man back out and Randy follows her. Mrs. Wilson goes over to the computer Randy and MaryAnn use and sits down.

I turn back to my drop files. I am looking for anything that would change an objects size. I am getting frustrated when Miss Penny calls my name. I turn around.

"Abby, could you come with me for a minute?"

"Sure." I answer and shut down the program I am using. I go out in the hall.

Miss Penny says nothing more but takes me back to the office where I registered. She directs me into a side office. Hailey is sitting, but Randy and MaryAnn are standing. Penny follows me into the room.

"Abby, this is the recreational center's director, Mr. McKay." Penny says.

"It's very good to meet you, Abby. Take a seat beside Hailey." He instructs.

I sit down. "Now I need to ask you some questions." Mr. McKay starts. "Why did you come to computer camp?"

"Hailey asked me to because she wanted someone in the computer camp she knew. I hadn't heard of the camp before she phoned." I answer honestly.

"What do you know about computers?"

"Just what Dad taught me," I frown, "he runs a one person web design company out of our basement."

"And you've spent a lot of time with your dad in the basement?" His voice makes it a question.

"Almost constantly before this school year," I pause, "when he studied or worked I often sat on his lap or on his second chair. He taught me to use his second computer so I wouldn't get bored."

"How many of the programs on the computers do you know?"

"I've seen all of them before, but I just realized I don't know everything about all the programs." I sigh. "I can't make the trees grow with Flash."

"So there is something you can learn about computers?" Mr. McKay smiles at me.

"There's always something to learn about computers they update programs all the time." I frown at him.

Mr. McKay laughs. "You're so very right? Now there's another question I need to ask. Did you lose your work when you came back from break today?"

"Yes and no." I take a deep breath. "It had been erased from the camper's work folder, but I brought a backup disk and saved on that so I still have it."

"Why did you bring a backup disk?" Mr. McKay frowns.

"Because my files were erased from the campers work folder twice yesterday, I brought a disk. If I am supposed to finish the computer game Randy wanted me to create then I knew I can't afford to start again every time I come in from break." I answer. "Not that it's going to get finished by Friday anyway, real computer games take months of work."

"How do you know that?"

"Because I helped Dad developed the concept for one then watched him build it. It took more than a week just to outline when and where all the different actions could possibly happen."

"Is there something you'd rather do?"

"I was thinking about working with Hailey but Randy said she needed to do a smaller project." I shrug. "She has good ideas."

Mr. McKay looks at Hailey. "Hailey, what did you want to do?"

"I wanted to learn to make a web site. Someplace I could put my stories and poems for people to read." Hailey answers.

"Now there's a good idea. Did you know, Abby, that Hailey has won writing contests?"

I shake my head.

"She wrote a story here at the centre that won first place and a hundred dollar prize." Mr. McKay beams. "We were all proud of her. Now you two go back to the computer lab and get started on that website while I have a talk with your instructors."

Hailey stands up and I follow her out of the room. "I hope this means I can give Travis back his computer."

"You really didn't want to make a computer game?" Hailey drops her voice to a whisper.

"A computer game is way too much work, most companies that make computer games have four or five people just doing the art work and I don't draw well." I answer back at a whisper.

Hailey giggles as we enter the computer room. Everyone looks at us. I go and gather my things, including my backup disk, then go back to my old desk. "You can have your computer back."

Travis almost looks as if he wants argue but then he changes his mind and moves. I sit down. "Now, what program do you want to use to do the web page?"

"What are my choices?"

"Word, Front Page, Dreamweaver, and Flash too but I already gave that computer away." I pause. "It depends what kind of backgrounds you want. There's ways to do screen movements in Dreamweaver."

"Things moving around makes it harder to read the writing."

"Okay." I consider that for a while. "We could do it just in Word, there's ways to save documents as web pages. How many poems and stories do you want to do?"

Hailey holds up a sheaf of handwritten papers.

"How fast do you keyboard?" I ask. Hailey shakes her head.

"Okay, you experiment with backgrounds and fonts while I enter these into the computer. I'll save it all on my disk so we'll know it won't disappear again." I take the papers.

By lunch I have about half of the papers on disk as most of her poems are short and she only writes one on a page. The stories are only a page or two. I even like some of them.

Randy and MaryAnn still haven't returned by lunch. Miss Penny comes and relieves Mrs. Wilson for the lunch period. She sits with us while we eat our lunch.

"Is Randy coming back?" Hailey asks.

"I don't know, Mr. McKay was still talking to Randy

and MaryAnn when I left."

"I hope we didn't cause them too much trouble." I sigh and set my tuna sandwich back on the table.

Penny looks at me for a long time before she asks. "Abby, how are you doing?"

"Better now I know I don't have to do a computer game all by myself."

"Yes, but are you learning something that you can use to make a project for Friday." Penny asks.

"I'm going to help Abby find something, right after we get my web site done." Hailey promises.

"How long should that take?" Penny asks.

"She doesn't want anything too complicated. We should be able to do most of the content by the end of the day, but then it just needs to be linked together and put up on a server." A slightly alarmed look enters Penny's eyes. "Or we could just save it to the disk and show it that way."

Miss Penny grabs on to the last solution. "Maybe it's better to leave it on disk we'll have to find some way to put it on a server later."

"Okay." I answer and pick up my sandwich again.

Hailey frowns without arguing.

We are just ending lunch when Randy and MaryAnn came back. Penny tells us good-bye and leaves. I get back to work after lunch and have everything entered by the break. We go outside for our break but MaryAnn comes with us, which she hasn't done all week.

Randy has her ref the soccer game while he coaches players. He leads us back inside and she follows behind. No one has tidied the room in between but it doesn't matter. Randy stops at our desks after break and watches for a moment. "It would be easier to edit and link in Dreamweaver." He says before moving on to the next student.

Hailey pauses. "What do you think? Would it be easier to edit?"

"It might." I agree. "You open Dreamweaver, I'll put the disk into your machine."

She opens the program. "You need to define the site." I point to show her where to click. The box opens. "What do you want to call the site?"

"Hailey's Writing."

"Okay. Type it in where it says site name." I direct. I pick up the papers and count them. "We're going to need fifteen, no sixteen pages. With Dreamweaver, you can make all the pages the same or every one different."

"Would it be too hard to make them all different?"

I shake my head. "We've got to define each one."

"How do you remember this stuff?"

"I've watched Dad do it so many times." I sigh. "Now open the site. Create sixteen new pages." I point to the screen and have her click through it. "Click here sixteen times." I point to the new page icon. I wait while she does that. "Now we have to click on each page and modify each one was it comes up. Start with the top one."

Hailey frowns. "Shouldn't you be doing this?"

"You're learning, I've set up pages for Dad before. Click on modify then page properties."

The box opens up. "Name the first one index. We'll list all the names of poems and stories on that one so people can choose which ones to read first. Then you have to choose a background or a background colour, a colour of the regular text, a colour for links and a colour for active links."

"Where do I get the backgrounds?" Hailey asks.

I sigh. "Dad said no to Internet access or we could find a free download site."

"My mom signed for me to use the Internet, but how do I find a free site?"

"You go to a search engine like google and type in what you want to find."

"Does that mean getting out of Dreamweaver?"

"No, you can have the Internet on at the same time Dreamweaver is open. Just open a new file and label it backgrounds because you'll have to save the background in the file to have the computer know where to look for it when you open the page."

Hailey dutifully opens a new file and labels it. I direct her and then I turn back to my own computer so I won't be breaking my promise to Dad. I am still trying to figure out what I can do for my project when I hear a long sigh from Hailey.

"What is it?"

"What if I only find one background that I really, really like?"

"You can use the same background for all the pages, some designers like to make all the pages look the same so surfers know it's all one site." I answer.

"But what if the words will disappear in the colours?" Hailey sighs again.

"We can put a white page layer on the background leaving the edges showing."

"Okay, how do I move this to my file?"

"Right click the mouse. Choose save as. A box should open up, click browse, and select a drive. Select Hailey's Writing, select background file and now click save. Now it should be right where you want it. Get out of the internet."

I take a breath. "Now open modify page properties. Select the background then close the box and the page that's open should show the background you like."

"Wow! It really worked." Hailey says so I finally look over. The background is bright with a flowery pattern. It isn't to my taste but it isn't my site.

"Now create a layer." I point to the tool bar.

"Can I try it on my own and only ask for help when I need it?" Hailey asks.

"Go right ahead. I'll go through the rest of the programs on the computer and see if I can find something to do for a project." I answer. "When you get them all ready I'll show you how to link them together."

I open PhotoShop and play for a while but it isn't any fun without images so I go to Illustrator and work there but I couldn't get my dinosaurs to look like real dinosaurs. I am relieved when Randy announces that camp is over for the day.

We start shutting down the computers. "Make sure you save before you get out of Dreamweaver," I instruct packing up my backpack. As soon as she does I take the disk out of the machine and give it to Hailey. "Hang onto your backup disk."

"Won't your father want it back?"

"Not once it's been in any of these machines. If I send something home, it will be by e-mail where any viruses can be filtered out."

"Oh." Hailey glances at the disk. "Could I get sick from it?"

"No, this kind of virus only affects computers." I try to hide the giggle that rises up inside me.

My laughter gets away from me. Hailey's face gets red. "I don't have a computer."

"Sorry." I immediately apologize. "If you don't have a computer then you don't have to worry about it."

She laughs at little herself. "We better go before Penny comes looking for us."

CHAPTER 8

Dad is in his office, but he has that don't bother me look he gets when he facing a tight deadline. "Can you make sandwiches for supper?" He asks when I peek around the corner.

I think about the sandwich I had eaten for today's lunch and the sandwich that would be for tomorrow's lunch but I say, "Yes." Like I said he usually doesn't ask me to do things so when he does, I feel horrible if I say no. I go upstairs and look in the cupboard. I find cans of tuna. I look through the fridge and to find cheese and peanut butter. I go back downstairs, "Tuna, cheese or peanut butter?"

The phone rings before Dad can answer. Instead, he picks up the phone. "Ted Hansen, One of A Kind Web Design."

Dad listens for a moment then takes a deep breath. "No, I can't get away right now." Dad waits another minute. "I'm busy, so you'll have to handle it yourself." He sets the phone down rather hard and stares at the computer screen.

I wait a long time then ask again, "Dad, tuna, cheese or peanut butter?"

"Peanut butter, toss on some banana then I won't have to think about dessert." He instructs. The phone rings upstairs. "Would you get that Abby, and tell whoever it is I can't talk right now."

Running back upstairs I grab the receiver, "Hansen residence."

"Abby, can I talk to your Dad?" It is Penny.

"He's busy, he said he didn't want to talk to anyone." I grimace at how bad that sounds. "He's really distracted with some work. He even asked for a peanut butter and banana sandwich for supper and he doesn't like peanut butter."

"Would he notice if you took say half an hour to make supper?"

"I doubt he'd notice."

"Okay, don't bother with the sandwiches I'll bring you something better," Penny announces.

I glance toward the stairs. I try to imagine Dad's reaction but I can't remember a single time someone brought us supper.

"Don't worry about anything Abby. I'll deal with your Dad."

I hang up the phone. Normally Dad would have been right up to find out who had called but not tonight. I frown and ask myself if I should tell him what she said. He doesn't want to be interrupted. I decide he'd find out soon enough.

I am torn between making Dad's sandwich and waiting for Penny. One minute I am reaching for the breadbox, the next I am withdrawing my hand hoping she will arrive before I start. Dad hates peanut butter; he argued against buying it. I am still arguing with myself when Penny arrives.

She knocks at the kitchen door instead of ringing the bell. When I answer it, she hands me a box then turns back to pick another two smaller boxes off the railing. She steps inside and places both those boxes on the table.

"I haven't told him you were coming." I whisper although, I am not certain why it is important for Dad not to hear me.

"Good," She whispers back taking the box from me she opens it and puts four smaller boxes in the freezer part of the fridge. Then she takes out a cake and a bowl of salad and sets them on the counter before pushing the bigger box aside. The she opens one of the smaller boxes, and unwraps the tin foil, underneath is a steaming hot roast beef dinner. She put a little salad on the side.

"Sit and eat." She instructs. She opens the other one and adds a larger portion of salad. I open the drawer and pull out cutlery. She takes a fork and knife along with the plate and goes downstairs. I start to take a bite, but I have to know what is happening.

I go to the top of the stairs then down just far enough to hear but not to see. "Here's your supper." I hear the plate being placed on the desktop.

"I told Abby I didn't…"

"Abby's a little girl who has had a rough day," Penny interrupts him. "She shouldn't have to be worried about a father who can't be bothered to find supper for himself let alone her. Eat, maybe you'll be able to think clearer, I doubt you've had a bite to eat all day."

"I made breakfast Abby never leaves the house without breakfast." Dad defends himself.

"And the last time you slept?"

"I'll sleep when I have time." I blink Dad doesn't

usually lose his temper. "I guess I am tired," He admits in a softer voice.

"Why do all this now?" Penny asks. "With Abby having time off..."

I hear a groan. "I was going to spend this week with Abby. There was some trouble and now everything is crazy. I know you think I'm a bad father..."

"You're not a bad father, you're a good parent but a tired one. Hailey is convinced you're the best father in the whole world." Penny interrupts to reassure him. "What you need is a meal and a good night's sleep."

"It's Abby's opinion that counts."

"She thinks you've lost it. You asked her for a peanut butter and banana sandwich for supper." There is a long silence.

"When she was little someone told me that the best way to avoid allergic reactions in children was not to feed them reaction provoking foods until they were older so I avoided buying peanut butter for years. Mrs. Martins gave Abby a peanut butter sandwich. Abby liked it and ask me to buy some. I told her it was disgusting and looked like baby poop. She said it was terrific baby poop so I finally gave in and bought a jar."

Penny starts laughing. "No wonder, poor Abby. Whatever prompted you to ask for a peanut butter sandwich?"

"The other options for sandwiches in this house right now are cheese and tuna and I've eaten almost nothing else all week." Dad answers but he sounds less tired.

"What if I offered to take Abby off your hands..."

"No." Dad immediately jumps on her suggestion.

"Listen to the end of what I have to say. I take Abby for the next two days. You get her back after the camp ends on Friday and you can come and visit any spare moment you have between now and then. I will make sure she gets three meals a day and goes to bed on time while you polish off this website."

"What do you get out of it?"

"I like Abby, Hailey likes Abby, and we get her company." Penny answers.

I bite my lip and go upstairs to eat. If Dad agrees, they can come up anytime and I want to have eaten enough that they don't know I was listening. They don't come until I am finished. I almost go to see what is keeping them but finally, they come up. Dad is carrying his finished plate.

"Abby, Penny is inviting to stay at her house until camp is over Friday." Dad doesn't smile or wink or give any of his standard signals as to whether he thinks this is a good idea. "Would you like to go?"

I don't know what to say, "Will you be all right here alone?" Is what finally comes out of my mouth.

"I'll be okay." Dad answers with a smile.

I ask."You won't let strangers in?"

"I promise to look before I open any door and to keep near the phone at all times." Dad answers solemnly.

I think it's a long time for being away from Dad but I like the idea having a chance to spend time with Penny. "I'd like to go, can I Dad?" I ask still not certain if he truly approves.

"Sure, go pack an overnight bag with three sets of clothes." He directs me by touching my shoulder so I know it is all right.

I go upstairs and take the bag I always took to Serena's. It has secret pockets, which is why Dad bought it. In those pockets, I have money, my own cell phone that is to be used only in emergencies and a special traveling toothbrush, a second hairbrush, small sized shampoo and my own soap. I pick out clean tee shirts, jeans, socks, underwear and pyjamas. I am all packed in under five minutes.

At the top of the stairs, I hear Penny say. "I will not take money for looking after Abby. She's a friend who's coming to stay for a couple of days."

My cheeks get red. I think for a moment then thump my way downstairs so they can hear me coming. Dad doesn't look happy. Penny wears the expression she has when she needs to separate talking girls in Sunday school class.

"Are you ready to go, Abby?" Penny asks as she takes my bag.

"I'm all packed." I cross over and hug Dad. He bends down to kiss my cheek. "Phone if there's any trouble."

"I will." I promise in the same whisper.

"The cake for dessert is on the counter, four homemade frozen dinners are in the freezer compartment, and there's more salad in the fridge, at least, please eat."

Dad blushes. "Wait a minute. I don't need you to feed me."

Penny is already ushering me out the kitchen door and she doesn't stop to argue with Dad. I hesitate. Penny urges me to continue. "You will see him at the computer camp showing on Friday."

I bite my lip. "I didn't give him the invitation."

"Then you'll have to tell him about when you phone every day to see how he's doing." Penny answers. "We need to get this bag to the van."

Penny unlocks her door and then opens the other door before she puts my bag in the back seat. "Sit up front with me there's something I need to tell you."

I get in the passenger door then belt myself in and

wait. Penny gets in and seat-belts herself in but she doesn't start the van. "Abby…" She starts and stops then takes a deep breath. "Hailey is my daughter, she lives with me."

"How come she doesn't call you Mom?" I frown and think about it. Hailey and Penny don't look alike not like Dad and me. Dad and me, we both have blond hair that looks red sometimes and green eyes. Penny has brown hair with blue eyes. Hailey has black hair and brown eyes.

"I never married her father and some of the kids at church teased her about not having a dad. She decided that if no one knew who her mother was then they won't ask about her father." Penny blushes.

"Dad didn't marry my mother either but I wouldn't ever call him anything but Dad."

"Well, certain children were very cruel." Penny sighs. "They used words that weren't very nice. Hailey admires you very much and she doesn't want you to know the bad things about her."

"Do I pretend I don't know you are her mother?"

"No, I'm not asking you to do that, it's just that Hailey pulls away when she's frightened. If you treat her as you've always treated her, then she'll realize that you haven't changed your attitude towards her."

Penny finally turns the key and her vehicle starts right away. I keep track of how far and which direction we drive. It isn't far. It is a small house with a large garage. Penny leads me in through the side door.

"Hailey, my father and I live here. Dad lives mostly in the garage and in the downstairs of the house. Hailey's and my rooms are upstairs." Penny explains as she leads me upstairs. "She's got twin beds in her room. You'll sleep there."

She walks down the hall to the end room. "We'll just

put your bag in there and then go find Hailey." She comes back out and leads the way down to the kitchen. "She must be out in the garage with her grandfather."

An idea strikes me. "She doesn't want me here, does she?"

"Hailey doesn't want you to know I am her mother." Penny sits on a chair. "Sit for a minute."

I sit. "Why did you want me to come?"

"Hailey has to realize that she can't lie to everyone about me." Penny starts.

"You want her to call you Mom."

Penny nods. "I don't want her to be ashamed of me." A tear makes its way down her cheek. "I thought if she could see how you and your Dad have worked things out."

"We don't talk about my mother if that's what you mean." I admit. "Except once, he wanted to make certain no one lied to me about what happened."

"Do you ever see your mother?" Penny asks softly.

"The judge took away her parental rights." I quote what Dad told me.

Penny sits in silence for a minute. "Is she that bad?"

I nod. "The judge ordered her and her father to stay away from me."

"Oh, my," Penny pauses. "She lives in town?"

"No, in a bigger city, the judge set strict rules about Dad keeping me, and one of them was he had to change towns and stay in school until he qualified for a good paying job. He still phones the judge every six months to report on how we're doing and to get his advice."

"Sounds like your dad turned his life around." Penny answers.

"I don't think Dad was bad." I frown "He just grew up in foster homes where he had to learn to look after himself. He's like Hailey he doesn't like people to think he's weak and needs help. Usually, he doesn't allow me to do any of the cooking, or cleaning, he does it all himself. He only did the focus group because I asked him and Bill Nessman decided they needed it."

"So, I had a mistake taking him supper?" Penny asks.

"You didn't give him a way to pay you back." I hesitate. "He would have felt better if you had."

"If he offers me help, of any kind, I'll accept." Penny promises. "Let's go look in the garage."

I follow her out to the garage. "My dad likes two things, fixing cars and listening to people's troubles. Hailey comes out here and tells him her troubles."

"Dad and I met him at church. He told Dad that fixing up his car would make it worth more."

"What did your Dad say?"

"Dad said he likes it as it is."

"What kind of car does your Dad drive?"

"An old one," I shrug. Penny laughs.

Penny is right; Hailey is sitting on a pile of old tires talking to her grandfather who is lying under a jacked-up car.

"Hi Dad," Penny calls.

"Hi Hailey, did you get all the pages done on the website?" I think maybe she might talk to me if I pick a subject she likes.

Hailey doesn't even look at me. Instead, she glares at Penny. "You had to tell her." Then she runs into the house.

I see tears in Penny's eyes. "I'll go talk to her." I race after Hailey and catch her before she can slam the bedroom door.

"You can't lock me out I'm sleeping in here." I block the door open.

"It's my room." Hailey stands up to me but I am not scared, the top of her head only comes up to my chin.

"Until Friday morning I get the other bed, Penny said so." I know from watching Dad deal with clients if I can get her to blink first I can win.

"You can go back to liking Serena. You can laugh together and call me a bastard." Hailey pushes tears off her cheeks with both hands.

"Then you can call me one back. My parents never married either." Hailey doesn't move for a minute. "In fact, I never want Dad to marry my mother." Hailey doesn't just blink she sits down on the bed as if her legs refuse to hold her up.

"How come you and Serena were friends?"

"Serena doesn't know anything about my mother. I wouldn't tell her or her mother." I shrug. "Dad told me not to tell anyone I didn't trust with the information."

"You don't think it makes me a horrible person?" Hailey sniffs.

"No, I don't." I answer and sit on the other bed. "But even if everyone in the world knew and called me nasty names I wouldn't stop calling Dad, Dad."

Hailey sniffs again but doesn't say anything.

"I'm going to talk to Penny." I get up and leave the room. I go down to the kitchen. Penny is sitting there crying. She tries to cover it up by blowing her nose but her eyes are red.

"I talked to her."

"And?"

"I left her to think about what I said." I sit down.

"And where did you learn to do that?"

"Dad, he's had to go to lots of counseling over the years, he's picked up a few tricks." I shrug. "So what do you to want to do now?"

"Play games." Penny suggests.

"What games?"

"Board games come and look at our collection." Penny leads me to a closet. It is full of boxes and I don't know enough about them to choose.

"What's your favourite?"

"Scrabble. You have to know lots of words and how to spell them." I think I grimaced because she changes ideas. "How about Yahtzee all you have to do is roll the dice?"

"Okay." I agree, not knowing either game.

Penny takes a box out of the cupboard and brings it to the table. "We each get a score card. We take turns rolling the dice and seeing what combinations we can get, we can roll all or some of the dice three times to try to get each combination. You'll learn as we go along." She laughs at what must be a puzzled look on my face.

We play nearly a whole game before Hailey comes into the room. She doesn't look upset anymore. "Can I play?"

"After a few more rolls," Penny nods.

Once Hailey starts to play, we don't talk about anything important.

Penny announces bedtime when the game breaks up. Hailey goes upstairs without saying anything. I hesitate.

"Do you want to phone your Dad and say goodnight?" Penny asks.

"Sure." I didn't know what else to say although I knew Dad didn't expect it.

"The phone is on the wall over there." Penny points to it. "Come upstairs when you're done."

I phone the office number. "Ted Hansen, One of A Kind Web Designs."

"Hi Dad, I just phoned to say goodnight." I don't

want him to worry. "Penny suggested it."

"She did, did she?" I can tell Dad is smiling. "How are you doing?"

"Okay I guess, Hailey's acting a little weird over having me here." I confess. "Penny told me that she's Hailey's mother. Hailey didn't want me to know. She thought I'd call her bad names."

"Give her a day to see you intend to treat her the same way as before." Dad suggests.

"That's about what Penny said."

"Then you're getting good advice. Don't worry, get a good night's sleep, and I'll either talk to you or see you tomorrow."

"I love you." I tell him.

"I love you too, Abby-girl. Tell Penny I said goodnight to her too." The phone goes dead so I hang up the phone and go upstairs.

I grab my stuff and go to the bathroom to get ready for bed. Penny is waiting when I get out. "Goodnight, Abby." She smiles.

I stop and give her a quick hug somehow she looks like she needs one. "Dad said to tell you goodnight."

"Oh." Penny's cheeks turn pink. "Hailey is already in bed. Do you need tucking in?"

"No." I answer. "Goodnight."

I go into the darkened room and get into bed. There is silence for a long time then Hailey says. "Penny doesn't like men hitting on her."

I frown at the picture that comes to mind. "Dad doesn't hit women."

Hailey sighs in a way I think is strange. "Not hitting women, hitting on women."

"I don't care, Dad doesn't do it. Goodnight." I roll over.

"All men do it." Hailey tells me. "Grandpa said so."

I don't answer. Instead, I remember Penny's pink cheeks. I hope she doesn't take Dad's message wrong.

"Abby." Hailey calls. "Abby."

"Let me go to sleep." I order. "Penny did something nice for Dad and he argued with her about it. He was just trying to say that he held no bad feelings towards her."

"Penny does nice things for people all the time." Hailey admits.

"She's a nice person," I tell Hailey. "She's also smart and lovely, and if she were my mom, I'd be proud to have everyone know it." This time, Hailey doesn't answer back so I take the opportunity to go to sleep.

CHATER 9

I wake up in a grump. I think it is because the sun is shining, the birds are singing but not only isn't my computer project not started but I am doing nothing about my math and I know Mr. Richter will find some way to give us that test. Friday seems so long ago that I am sure that Monday morning is going to come soon. I dress and go down to breakfast.

Penny looks like she is ready to cry, her father seems stiff, only Hailey seems happy. "My grandmother is coming to visit." I can almost see bubbles coming off her as she speaks.

"Dad, how could you?" Penny words come out almost as a plea. "Not here."

"I didn't sell the house. The judge gave her half of everything. I'd rather she didn't bring him here, but she does have that right." He mutters back.

"Abby, do you want some cereal?" Penny asks when she finally notices me.

I just nod. Somehow I have a longing for one of

Dad's hugs so I go over and hug Penny but somehow it isn't the same. For a split second, Penny hugs me back then she breaks away to find a bowl and some corn flakes. That cereal sticks in my teeth but I don't want to make her find something else so I just eat them and go back upstairs to find my toothbrush.

"Abby, are you ready to go?" Penny calls up the stairs.

"Be there in a minute." I go to the bedroom and slip the cell phone into the pockets of my jeans. I want to call Dad but there is no time right now. I head downstairs.

"Here's your lunch." She hands me a brown bag.

"I forgot my backpack at home." I suddenly realize the fact.

"Add it to Hailey's bag, we don't have time to stop this morning." Penny answers. "We'll visit your dad after camp today."

"Okay," I answer and give it to Hailey who puts it in her backpack. I get in the back seat of the van without saying another word. Penny glances back at me to see if I have my seatbelt done up. I meet her eyes and she looks scared, then she immediately looks away so I can't see.

Once we get to the recreational centre, Hailey springs out of the car. I get out more slowly. Penny pauses. "Did I do something wrong, Abby?"

"It's not you, it's math and computer camp."

"Computer Camp, I understand but what's this about math?" Penny asks as she leads the way inside.

"I got in trouble at school on Friday for not being able a math problem. I think the teacher is going to give us a test and I haven't figured out how to deal with it." I report. "Dad sent me to camp to get my mind off it." Penny gives me a very strange look but opens a door to an office and shows me where to sit down. "He thought I was just too upset when I tried to do the problem and that my mind remembers the feeling I got trying to do the math and shuts down." I felt compelled to defend him.

"He thought you should take a break from it." Penny interprets. "You are having a hard time with the computer stuff?"

"I know too much to do the easy stuff but not enough to do the really hard stuff. I draw stick figures, not real pictures and find it difficult to dream up original stories." I sigh. "I'd rather be home doing novel study."

Penny actually laughs. "Abby, sometimes you are so funny."

"If I haven't said I was bored, I could be setting up files and doing all the background stuff for Dad. Not that he can't do it himself but, at least, I'd have a job."

"You like helping him?"

"I'm a helper, not an artist. Dad's the artist. Everybody expects kids to be artists. Dreaming up new ideas is hard work."

"Maybe adults want you to try to be the artist before you settle for being a helper. They want you to take the time to search for what's inside you." Penny suggests. "If deep down you really like to be a helper that will still be there once you have tried to dream up something new."

I sigh again. "I better go help Hailey link her pages into a site." I stand and reach for the door.

Penny speaks before I turn the knob. "Abby, why do you think your Dad told you to tell me goodnight?"

"Because I told him you suggested that I phone and say goodnight. I never did it when I stayed at Serena's. I was scared he might think something was wrong if I didn't tell him why I phoned." It seems like a long explanation but I am scared I mixed something up.

"Then all he meant was goodnight?"

I just nod.

"Okay, you go help Hailey with her website." She smiles. I leave the room and then take a deep breath. I am late getting to computer camp but no one says a word to me.

Hailey has all of her pages together. "Where did you go?"

"I talked to Penny." I answer. "Are you ready to start linking?"

She frowns. "Penny isn't your mother."

"No, but she is my Sunday school teacher and I'm staying at her house." I look at one of her pages. "You need to add a back to menu at the bottom of each page otherwise, they will only link one way."

"I don't want to type it sixty million times." Hailey snaps.

"Then type it once and copy/paste it to the rest of the pages." I suggest. "Or people will get to the end of that poem and not know where to go if they want to read more of your writing."

She says nothing more but sets to work. I open the file with my dinosaurs from the camper work file, I haven't thought it worth saving to the backup disk, and try to make the shapes look more like dinosaurs. I move lines, bend lines and then erase lines and start over because they still look nothing like dinosaurs.

"What now?" Hailey asks.

"Go to the index page. Highlight the name of the first poem. Go over to the toolbar and select the link button. Now see the box at the bottom of the page. There is a place for the link name, go browse. Select the page that poem is on so it comes up in the link box and you've done your first link. Now go to the bottom of that page and highlight back to menu now select link from the toolbar. Browse until you find the index page. Do that for all the pages." I never even look up from my screen.

"Abby, are you mad at me?" Hailey ask.

"I'm never going to have a project ready for Friday." I open the edit drop menu select everything and then the delete button. "I wish I had never come here."

"Everyone, it's time for the break. Save, shut down and line up at the door." Randy announces. I turn off the computer with a sigh and then go stand in line.

Hailey moves slower, in fact, she doesn't get into line at all. She says something to MaryAnn instead and leaves the room.

When we get to the field, Randy announces we would play a form of softball. Everyone but one person gets a place in the outfield. The one person is the batter, he or she gets three strikes or he or she got a hit after which the batter would run to first base and back. Then the batter moves to outfield and the back catcher gets to be batter and pitcher moves to back catcher until everyone rotates around. I start in the left field.

I wait for Hailey to appear but she doesn't. The harshness of my words bothers me. I sigh deeply then someone yells. The ball plops to the ground beside me; I pick it up and throw it to a girl closer to home base. She turns and throws it to someone else but by the batter is already back at home and Randy calls for us to rotate. I move to center field.

Travis yells. "Butterfingers; what was an easy fly ball. Get off the field if you're not going to play."

I am grumpy enough to call out but I've already hurt Hailey so I think better of it instead I turn and run up to the top of some wooden seats. Then I do what I've ached to do all morning I sit down and phone Dad.

"Ted Hansen, One of a Kind Web Designs."

"Hi, Dad," The long sigh that follows tips him off.

"What's the problem, Abby?"

"Everything, I'm having a grumpy day."

"How about starting with your top five concerns?" Dad laughs.

"We're supposed to do projects for a showing on Friday and I can't think of anything to do. Hailey's grandmother is coming to town and Penny is scared. I said something to upset Hailey because of my mood, now I feel bad about it. I'm not working on my math and I'm sure Mr. Richter will find a way to give us that test. I need a hug from you but I won't get to see you 'til Friday." I stopped and counted on my fingers. "Is that five or six?"

"Too many for a nine-year-old." Dad teases then he gets serious. "First you can design a personalized calendar that will tell me at least two days in advance that my daughter has a showing on Friday so I know to work fast enough to be there." I can almost see him ticking the first one off on his fingers. "Two; are you sure Penny was scared?"

"Penny asked her dad not to let her mother come but Mr. Whitfield said that her mother still owned half of everything and she had the right to come, even if she brought him. I don't know who 'him' is." I report. "How can someone own half of everything?"

"Two: don't you say anything about what you heard to anyone else including Hailey." Dad's voice gets soft like when he gets upset. "Three: apologize to Hailey. Four: I want to talk to someone before you stress yourself out over the math. You're trying to convince yourself of something that is simply not true and I have to find some way to stop it before it becomes a real problem. Five: I'll make certain we see each other long before Friday."

"I didn't mean to upset you." I feel like crying.

"It's okay, Abby." His voice returns to nearer normal, "It's just sometimes adults say things to each other that children shouldn't hear and I think that was one of them. You just think about making me a calendar and leave me to deal with the adult things."

"In what colours?"

"Light brown and blue." Dad comes back quickly, "With pockets, like blue jeans and lists that move upward instead of down."

"Anything else?"

"Yes, I want a place to get regular notes from my daughter so I know what's she's worrying about so I can do something before she works herself in a grump."

I finally have to smile. "Oh Dad, I love you."

"I love you too." Dad answers. "Go show them what you can do."

I turn off the cell phone, stand and slipping it into my pocket. "Abby, breaks over." Randy calls. I run down to join the group.

Hailey is sitting at her computer waiting for the class of start. I stop beside her. "Hailey, I was wrong to take my grumpy mood out on you. I was just having a hard time with what I was trying to do but I have a whole different idea now. You can ask me anything you need to."

"Penny said I should be asking Randy or MaryAnn. They get paid to answer my questions."

"Can you remember what I told you about linking?" I ask. She nods. "Then go ahead and after that, you can pretty it up."

"Isn't it pretty enough?" Hailey's cheeks darken.

"Sorry, I use Dad's terms for things sometimes. I mean put a title on the index page. Say something about yourself like how you won that prize and how long you've been writing. You know add whatever details you think will get people interested in reading your website."

"Oh." Hailey smiles, "That kind of stuff."

"While you do that I have to start all over again." I roll my eyes. "What's new?"

Hailey releases a little giggle, which tells me I've succeeded in fixing our friendship.

I sit down and start picking out colours. I find an almost tan colour before I find blue jean blue. I put them together I smile. I'd seen a book cover, a western novel in the library with just those colours. The thought of Dad wearing a cowboy hat and riding a horse pops into my head and I have to stifle a giggle. Suddenly this project is fun.

Lunch comes and goes; I eat an apple while I work but never notice the other food until Hailey brings it to my attention. In fact, I miss the call when Randy calls for the afternoon break and MaryAnn comes over to my desk to tell me that I have to go outside with the rest of the campers. Even while I get closer to the infield in the continuation of the softball game I am thinking about just how I am going to make everything work. Randy frowns at me once for not making a play but I just grin back at him.

It is the change in the noise level in the room that alerts me to the end of the day. I look up to see the other kids pack up. Then I notice the silence.

"This is the computer camp?"

I immediately turn, "Dad!" I don't remember leaving my seat but I do remember wrapping my arms around his neck and being lifted into the air.

"Are you ready to go? I phoned Penny and asked if I could pick you two up and meet her at the river park."

Dad looks at Hailey and winks.

"As soon as Abby saves and backs up her work." Hailey giggles.

I almost jump out of Dad's arms to get back to my computer and get everything ready to leave for the day. For a second I felt like all my troubles were finally over then, I remembered my math book and opening it Sunday morning. "Can I see what you're working on Abby-girl?" Dad asks.

"No, you have to come on Friday if you want to see." I tease.

"You mean I have to skip that contract in Saudi Arabia on Thursday?" Dad teases right back.

"You're going away?" Hailey's eyes grow big.

Dad sobers right up. "No, I am teasing Abby. I never meant to upset you, Hailey."

"Oh." Hailey answers. "I'd let you see my website but I already shut down my computer."

"I would be honoured to see your work." Dad tells her. "In fact, I promise to come back on Friday to see both your works of art."

I smile at Dad's teasing but I am careful not to let Hailey see. I shut off the switch. "Okay, we can go." I announce and grab Hailey's backpack. "Race you to the jalopy."

"Jalopy, what kind of car is it?" Hailey asks Dad.

"A 1968 Olds," Dad answers while ushering her into the hall.

"That's not a jalopy." Hailey calls to me. "It's a classic."

"Unfortunately," Dad corrects. "It's both." I turn back to see if Dad was smiling, but what I see is MaryAnn standing in the hall watching Dad and Hailey. Randy comes out and says something to her. She ignores him.

Randy frowns at her.

"I bet I can beat you out to the car." I challenge Hailey knowing that it will get Dad away from there faster.

"I will take that bet." Dad scoops Hailey into his arms as he says. "No running in the halls, Abby." I stride to the car. I know he'd get there first. He can walk fast, taking long steps, but I am not too far behind. Hailey is back on the ground before I arrive.

Dad opens the back door of the car. "Hansen taxi service, all passengers in the back seat."

"Penny lets me ride up front." Hailey starts to protest.

"It's safer if you ride in the back." Dad answers in his, I'm not going to change my mind, voice.

"Come on." I grab her hand. "Dad likes to play chauffeur. It makes him think he's got celebrities in the car if we ride in the back."

Dad bends down and kisses my cheek. "When you're here I've always got special passengers."

I hustle Hailey into the car. "This way we can whisper behind his back." I speak in a low voice.

"What sort of things can we whisper?" Hailey wants to know once we are in and buckled up. Dad winks at me in his mirror and I know he hears me.

"About how he's ancient but doesn't look it." I answer and see Dad wrinkle his nose. "Or how…" I am trying to think of something really outrageous. "He snores and talks in his sleep."

Hailey looks at Dad. "Is that true?"

I can't help but laugh. Hailey looks hurt and I am immediately sorry. "No Hailey, but I like to tease him. The truth is he likes his tuna bone dry and he thinks peanut butter is baby poop."

This time, Hailey laughs. "Abby, you're teasing again."

I laugh with her simply to let her think I am joking

again.

The trip down to the river only takes a few minutes. Penny is pacing by her already parked van when we pull into the lot. Dad parks in the next space. From my side of the car, I can see my bag on the backseat.

"Ted, can we talk while the girls play?" Penny asks before Dad even gets all the way out of the car. She is twisting her key chain in her fingers.

"Sure, Abby, stay on the closer equipment where I can see you." Dad instructs. I nod and run to the nearest set of monkey bars, Hailey follows. She goes in and out and round and round. I go to the top where I can watch Dad and Penny.

Dad leans against our car with his arms folded across his chest but Penny can hardly stand still. She rocks back and forth to the point she has to shuffle her feet once to remain standing. After that, Dad puts his hand out to steady her. I glance down to see if Hailey is watching but she is concentrating on her climbing. I watched for a little while longer suddenly Dad reaches out to put an arm around Penny's shoulder and turns her to face away from us. I grab tight to the bars. Dad never touches other adults, and then I see him rub her shoulder and realize that he is comforting her, I breathe a sigh of relief.

"Abby." Hailey calls and I climb down to where she is. I don't want her to think my Dad is hitting on her mother. I am careful not to look towards the cars but move to the side of the bars away from them. After a while I hear a door shut and look over, Dad stands behind the car like he has just put something in the trunk. Penny seems calmer as she gets into her van and drives off.

"Girls, we're going over to our place for supper. Penny's gone to get some things then she coming to join us."

"Dad, there's nothing at home to eat." I remind him.

"Penny is going to stop at the grocery store." Dad answers, "Now."

I start towards the car, Hailey follows but this time, she doesn't say anything about getting into the back seat. She waits until we were moving. "I thought you had a big contract." She speaks loud enough for Dad to hear.

"Some things are more important than contracts. How would you like to stay with Abby for a few days?" Dad asks.

"I thought she was staying at my house?" Hailey frowns.

"Your grandfather is having company and he needs your room for someone else to stay in so you and your mom are staying with us." Dad explains.

"My grandmother is coming." Hailey pauses then frowns.

I look up to catch Dad's expression in the mirror but there is nothing on his face to show how he is feeling. "Yes, and your mom doesn't think they have enough space because your grandmother is bringing someone else with her. They need both bedrooms."

"Oh." Hailey leans back in her seat and frowns slightly. "Abby, do you want me to stay?"

"It'll be fun." I respond to the look Dad gives me through the mirror.

"But will I get to see my grandmother?" Hailey asks.

"That you have to discuss with your mom." Dad tells her. Hailey sighs deeply.

After we get enter the kitchen door, Dad says. "Hailey will be in the bedroom next to yours. Take her up and show her around, I have to get your bag out of the car."

I nod. "Come on." I lead the way upstairs.

"Why don't I stay in your room?" Hailey asks.

"Because I only have a single bed." I answer then try to reassure her. "We'll spend all our time together."

The room next to mine has, all the same, furniture my room does; a single bed, a desk and a dresser. The walls are a soft yellow because Dad doesn't like white or off-white, he calls those institutional colours, and the curtain has a sunflower pattern on it.

Hailey stands in the middle of it for a minute and just looks around. I hear Dad open and close my bedroom door then he steps in the room with us. "Will it do?"

"It's pretty." Hailey nods. "Where will Penny sleep?"

"Your mom will have the bedroom on that side of you." Dad points to the opposite side from mine.

"Where's your room?"

"Across the hall from Abby's, the bathroom is across from yours and the library is across from your mom's." Dad answers.

"You have a library?" Hailey's jaw drops.

"Get Abby to show it to you, I have to go down and set the table for supper."

I pick up the suggestion and take Hailey down to see our library, although calling it that is really a joke. When Dad was renovating, he asked me what I wanted since we had lots of spare bedrooms. I said a place to read. The library was the result. Every possible inch of the walls is devoted to bookshelves.

Most of them are empty; I have one long shelf half-full of every book I ever owned. Dad doesn't read a lot of story-type books and he has bookshelves downstairs in his office for his computer manuals and business books.

I lead Hailey in then I wait for her to question the lack of books. "Awesome." Hailey turns around and around. "Just think of all the books you can buy and never have to give one away."

I sit in the big lounge chair; it and its footstool are the only other furniture in the room. Hailey is in raptures. She dances around the room looking at every empty shelf even the ones you have to bend down to see.

After about two minutes of watching her, I start to get bored. "Do you want to see my room?"

Hailey stops and looks up. "Can I see Penny's room first?"

"Sure." I shrug my shoulders and walk across the hall. The room has the same furniture as the other two but the walls are green and the curtain has leaves on it.

"I think I like mine better." Hailey announces. I lead her down the hall to my room. It is apricot with white lace curtains; my stuffed toys and stuff make it more lived in.

"Abby, Hailey, could you come down here?" Dad calls.

"Come on." I say and head downstairs.

Penny is there but she has been crying. She is putting food in the fridge. "I'll cook."

"No, Abby, give Penny a tour of the house while Hailey and I put some supper together." Dad gives me a look.

Penny looks like she might start to cry again so I reach for her hand. "Come see my library." I pull her out of the room and up the stairs. "Don't worry about Hailey all he'll let her do is rip up the lettuce for salad." I lead her all the way down the hall to the end. "This is the library." I open the door. "It was Dad's idea of a joke when I asked for some place to read. Hailey really likes it."

Penny looks around but I don't think she sees it. I drag her across the hall. "This is where you're staying." This time, she starts to cry.

I hesitate then ask. "What's wrong?"

She looks at me. "It's too hard to say."

"Then why don't I show you the bathroom so you can wash your face before Hailey starts asking questions?" I take her across the hall. Penny follows. I stay outside and let her have some privacy. She seems a little better when she comes out.

"Across there is Hailey's room, mine's next to it. This one is Dad's but I never go in there." I open the door so she could see where Hailey is staying, and then my room. I don't open Dad's. "What's all of the upstairs?" I lead the way back down to the kitchen but I take a sharp turn at the bottom. "This way is the living room."

Penny stops for a moment to watch Dad and Hailey. Dad is at the stove. Hailey is at the opposite counter making salad. I reach for her hand and she follows me.

"Dad buys movies, but only ones that a nine-year-old should watch." I show her the entertainment unit. A formal dining area comes off one end so it is a big room. The kitchen fills in the rest of this floor.

"Downstairs from here is Dad's office and downstairs from there is the furnace room and Dad's workshop." I don't know if I should take her down there.

"Abby, Penny, supper's on." Dad calls. I head for the kitchen.

Dad serves a stir-fry with Chinese noodles. I watch Dad's eyes figure out where he want me to sit. Hailey is already in my usual place. Dad sits Penny next to him and serves her first. I sit around the corner from Penny.

Everything is very tense at first. Penny stares downward at her plate but doesn't pick up her fork. I decide the best thing to do might be to concentrate on eating.

Hailey frowns after I'd taken my first bite.

"Grandfather always says grace."

Dad's eyebrow gives a sudden twitch. Penny turns red. I try to think of something to say but my mind goes blank. Dad comes to the rescue. "Sorry Hailey, how about if you pray for us tonight?"

Hailey bites her lip then bows her head. "Our heavenly Father, we thank you for your provision. We ask that you bless our use of it and we ask for your protection. Amen." She recites.

I hear Penny whisper "Amen."

"Hailey, are you going to design websites for a living?" Dad asks to fill in the silence.

"No, I'm going to be a writer." Hailey announces. "I'm putting poems and short stories on the site I'm building at camp."

"Wouldn't it be better to publish them as a book?" Dad asks. "People buy books. If your stories are on a website, then people don't have to pay to read them. You don't make any money that way."

Hailey twists noodles on her fork. "But if I don't put them on the web, how will enough people know if they want to read them?"

There is another silence, this time, I think of something. "Maybe what you should do is put some of your best stories and poems on the website now then when people get to know your work you can write new stories and publish them in books."

"It might work but people don't like to start paying for something they used to get for free." Dad answers. "You might be better off selling your stories to some of the e-zines or even paper magazines. People look there for stories by new writers. A stand alone website can be difficult for people to find."

"Oh." Hailey frowns. "How do I find places to sell my

writing?"

"Well, if you and your mother stick around until after I get my current website done, I'll do some research and show you." Dad promises.

Hailey nods and gets down to eating her supper. Penny glances at Dad then down at her plate. I shift my concentration to eating. The rest of the meal is silent. When everyone but Penny is finished, Dad stands up and goes to the counter.

"I still have some cake if anyone wants dessert." Dad announces. "I'm going to have to get back to work. Abby can show you where everything is."

"I'll do the dishes," Penny tells him. Dad cuts the cake, serves himself a slice then sets the cake on the table with clean small plates before taking his piece and going downstairs.

I serve Hailey then myself. "Penny, do you want some?"

"I'll serve myself." Penny tells me. "You two eat up and go watch a movie."

"Okay. The dish soap is under the sink."

"I'll find it." Penny assures me.

I take Hailey into the living room and let her choose the movie. She squeals when she sees the selection and takes forever picking one out. I get tired of watching her and peep back in the kitchen. Penny is sitting at the table her head on her arm. I think she is crying. I want to go ask her what is wrong but then remember she said about it being too hard to talk about. I return to watching Hailey agonize over which movie to watch.

Finally, I run out of patience. "Haven't you made up your mind?"

"I don't get to watch many movies." Hailey frowns. "There's, at least, four here I really, really want to watch."

"You'll be here a few days so pick out four and we'll watch one a night." I suggest.

"But which one first?" Hailey frowns.

"You close your eyes I'll mix them around and then you can pick one at random." I answer. "Or it will be passed bedtime before we get to see one."

My warning seems to call her to action because the next thing I know, she's picked out a pirate movie and wants me to put it in the video machine.

The movie is just over when Penny comes in and announcing bedtime. I go upstairs and get ready for bed without saying anything. Hailey doesn't follow me straight up. I am between the covers when someone knocks on the door.

"Come in." I call thinking it might be Penny. Dad opens the door.

"Do you need a bedtime snack?"

"Nope, I ate enough supper. I could use a good night hug."

Dad comes over and gives me a hug. I hug him back. "Abby-girl, you've been a good sport about it but do you really mind having Penny and Hailey here?"

I think about it for a minute because I know Dad isn't going to take any non-thinking answers. "I really like Penny. She's really nice. Hailey so full of energy she can be exciting to be around. I don't mind having them here. I just wish there was someway to keep Penny from being so sad."

Dad sigh. "I think the best way to do that is to keep Hailey occupied so she forgets about visiting her grandmother."

"Why wouldn't Penny want Hailey to see her grandmother?" I frown.

"It's not her grandmother exactly..." Dad sigh. "It's a

long story and not one you need to hear. The end result is her grandmother has a friend Penny doesn't want Hailey to meet."

"Oh." I bite my lip. "Could we invite her grandmother without her friend?"

"It would be impolite to not ask him without a reason." Dad shakes his head.

I sigh, "It's just too complicated."

"I feel that way sometimes too." Dad answers. He hugs me again then kisses my forehead. "Try to get a good night's sleep."

"Night, Dad." I slip down between the covers.

CHAPTER 10

It is just starting to get light out when I first open my eyes then I hear it again. Thumping on the front door. I get up and go to the window; Pastor Ben and Mr. Whitfield are out there. I go across the hall and lightly tap on Dad's door but when I hear movement, it is from downstairs. Then I hear Dad's voice.

"There's no need to wake up the entire house."

"Where's Penny?" Pastor Ben asks.

"Upstairs, last bedroom on the left-hand side." Dad answers.

"Then you're not denying that she's here?" Roger Whitfield demands.

"No, Penny and Hailey are both here." Dad answers softly. "I didn't think she or her daughter would be safe in her own bed considering the circumstances."

Pastor Ben cuts in. "Why would she think that?"

"Kimberly and her husband are coming to stay. Penny got all upset about it." Mr. Whitfield reports, "But not enough to do something this drastic."

"I always thought Penny had a good head on her shoulders. Yes, she made a mistake once but moving in with a man is out of character for her." Pastor Ben's voice isn't as deep or as even as it is from the pulpit Sunday morning.

"Considering her mistake was trusting her parents." Dad interjects.

"What are you insinuating?" Mr. Whitfield's voice rises.

"Penny was molested by her stepfather. She doesn't want her daughter subject to the same treatment." Dad answers.

A sound like a chair being scraped across the floor comes first then there was a plop. "Are you certain?" Pastor Ben's voice sounds strange.

"Penny is what twenty?"

"Nineteen." The pastor supplies.

"Hailey is nine. That mean's Penny was ten when Hailey was born," Dad answers.

"Hailey's eight, her birthday is at the end of the year." Pastor Ben says, "I'd never thought about it that way."

"My ex-wife still owns half my house. I can't legally keep them away."

"A DNA test would prove it one way or the other." Dad states softly. "Jail time would keep them away."

"Except then none of us will have a place to live." Mr. Whitfield answers.

"Is your house more important than your daughter and granddaughter?" Dad's voice is as soft as I have ever heard it.

I hear footsteps behind me. I glance back upstairs to find Penny standing two steps above me with her mouth hanging open. I stand up and take her hand. "Take me back to bed."

"No, I have to face the pastor." Penny whispers.

"Dad will talk to him." I whisper. Penny shakes her head then releases her hand and continues downstairs. I hesitate not certain whether I should follow her down or go back to bed.

"Ted, Abby's wake." Penny says "She needs you."

"Abby." Dad calls. I go downstairs. "I've got the databases up and running but I need some advice on what names to put on them."

I go over and take his hand. "We'll be downstairs if you need us." Dad tells Penny.

Penny nods and sits at the table with Pastor Ben while her father stares into the dark glass of the kitchen window.

Dad shows me the web pages with the entrances to databases. I have no memory of any advice I give him. I fall asleep in his lap.

I wake up in my bed. I get up and dress before I realize the house is silent. I go to the kitchen but it is empty. "Is anyone here?" I call out.

"Downstairs." Dad calls back.

I go down to his office. "Where are Penny and Hailey?"

"They went to the recreational center. I said I'd bring you along once you woke up. Eat something and I'll take you over." Dad gives me a hug.

"Dad, are Penny and Hailey still staying here?" I bite my lip.

"Pastor Ben advised Penny to stay here until they could find another safe place." Dad answers. "I think we still have them for a few days."

I nod and go upstairs. I find some muffins in the breadbox and eat those. Dad comes up while I am eating them.

"What about lunch?" I ask.

"Penny said she'd pack some for you with hers and Hailey's. Are you ready to go?"

"Are you sure you're not too tired to drive?" I notice circles under his eyes.

"I'm a computer programmer, we're trained to go without sleep." Dad winks.

"Which is why so many new programs have bugs." I guess. Dad laughs.

I get there just as the other campers are going on break. Randy frowns when he sees me. "Get in line."

"Can't I just work on my project? I don't want to run out of time." I ask.

"I'll stay with her." MaryAnn volunteers.

Randy's frown deepens. "I suppose." He doesn't look happy but I ignore that and sit down at my computer.

MaryAnn moves to where she can see that I am doing. "What are you doing?" She asks.

"Making a personalized calendar for my father." I answer and start by checking where I left off.

"Your dad's rather special, isn't he?"

I don't like the way she says it but I clamp my mouth shut when the thought to tell her that Penny is staying with us crosses my mind. "He's my Dad." Is what I say.

"What's your mom like?"

I bite my tongue and try to think of something that will put an end to her questions but nothing comes. I know that if she leaves the room I will have to leave and I need to work on my project so I do not want to say anything outrageous. I chose something bland.

"She's just a mom." I shrug.

"I suppose they're wildly in love." It isn't quite a

question so I choose not to answer. MaryAnn pauses. "Is your mom going to be here on Friday?"

"She doesn't live in town." I shake my head.

"Oh." MaryAnn smiles. I don't like her smile. It is sort of a half-smile with knowing look behind it. She goes back to her desk, which I want. I work steadily until lunch break when Penny comes in with food for Hailey and me. She delivers it and leaves again without meeting my eyes.

"How's the website going?" I ask.

"I thought you'd forgotten about me?" Her bottom lip bulges.

"No, but if I don't keep my full concentration on my programming, I'm going to start making mistakes." I explain. "Then it won't work as I want."

"Penny's acting funny." Hailey frowns. I don't know what to say. "Is your Dad acting funny too?"

I think about it for a few minutes. "He usually is like this when he's got lots of work."

"Oh." Hailey sags like a balloon burst inside her.

Randy comes over. "How are the projects going?"

"I'm done." Hailey reports.

"I've still got work to do." I answer.

"Then, Hailey, how about if you help MaryAnn and me? We need some decorations made for tomorrow's show."

Hailey nods. "She needs to concentrate."

I finish my lunch and go back to work. Randy gives me the option of working through my break and I take it. My eyes are sore by the time Penny comes to get us.

Penny takes one look at me. "Your eyes are red."

I shrug. "I worked through the break. I'm way behind on my project. Dad does it all the time."

"Your dad is an adult and is entitled to make such decisions. You are a child, and Randy and MaryAnn are responsible for your well-being." Penny frowns. "You are supposed to have breaks from the computer."

"Okay, tomorrow I'll take my breaks." I offer, knowing that I still may be able to get my project done because I've managed to finish the major stuff today.

"I should report them." Penny asks.

"Can you take me home first so I can rest my eyes?" I ask hoping she won't think it worth the bother of returning tonight.

"Abby's Dad will wonder what's keeping us." Hailey comments.

"Oh, alright." Penny gives in. "Out to the van."

Hailey runs ahead while I stay closer to Penny. We are almost out the door when Mr. McKay steps out of an office. "Penny, can I speak to you for a minute?" He asks.

Penny hands me her keys. "Wait for me in the van."

I take the keys and go to find Hailey. We get into the vehicle and wait a long time for Penny to appear.

When she finally appears, she doesn't say anything instead opens the backdoor and sets down a cardboard box. Then she slides in behind the steering wheel and sits there. She says nothing and doesn't move to start the van. I glance in the mirror and think she looks pale but her eyes are looking straight ahead so I can't see them.

"Penny, here are your keys." I hold them out. She doesn't move but instead just kept staring straight ahead. I jingle them without getting a response.

Hailey turns to me her eyes seem larger than normal. "What happened?"

"I don't know." I frown. "Penny?" I call. No reaction.

I reach into my pocket and pull out my cell phone. I punch in Dad's number.

"Ted Hansen..."

"Dad, it's Abby. Penny's acting weird." I interrupt his

greeting.

"Tell me." Dad answers.

"We were coming out of the building and her boss asked her to talk to him. Later she came out of the building with a box. She stopped to open the back and put the box in before she sat in the driver's seat. Now she is staring straight ahead not moving. I offered her keys back and she didn't even move."

"Whatever you do don't give her the keys." Dad instructs. "I'll be there as soon as I can."

"Thanks, Dad." I answer then put the cell phone back in my pocket.

"What did he say?" Hailey whisper loudly.

"He's coming." I answer trying to sound reassuring. "Why don't you try calling her?"

"Penny!" Hailey calls.

"Call her mom." I instruct. "She wants you to call her mom."

"I never call her mom." Hailey answer.

"Try it," I command.

"Mom!" Hailey cries out. Penny still doesn't waiver.

"We'll just have to wait for Dad." I lean back in my seat and take steadying breaths. I close my eyes for a few minutes continuing to concentrate on my breathing.

"Penny?" Randy calls out from right next to the van. I nearly bump my head on the ceiling. "Penny, why haven't you left?"

Penny still doesn't move. Just then I hear a siren, it gets closer as Randy leans on the window. "Penny!" He waves his hand in front of her face.

"Don't touch her. Penny doesn't like to be touched." Hailey crawls into Penny's lap to push him away.

Dad arrives seconds before the ambulance. "Girls, go sit in my car. You are going home with me."

I get out and hand Penny's keys to Dad. "She didn't even move when Hailey crawled on her lap."

Hailey and I go sit in Dad's car while the men from the ambulance put Penny on a stretcher and place her in their vehicle. Dad stays right beside her until they pull away. Randy and MaryAnn talk to Dad for a minute then he comes back to the car.

"Is Penny going to be all right?"

"I don't know," Dad answers. "Let's hope the doctors can do something for her." Mr. McKay comes out of the building. Dad looks at the man and Mr. McKay starts toward us.

"We need to pray for your Mom." I tell Hailey. She nods, bows her head and whispers to her petition to Jesus.

I release a long breath close my eyes and start my own plea for Penny. We are still praying when I hear Dad's voice. I open my eyes.

"I didn't have any choice. The word came down from the board to recheck old applications. There were lies about her qualifications on her job application." Mr. McKay stands toe to toe with Dad. "Her father used his connections to get her the job to begin with, maybe he had a falling out with his contact on the board."

Dad steps away to come over and slide into the driver's seat. "I'm going to take you home then go up to the hospital."

"Can't we go see my mother?" Hailey asks.

"I would like to hear what the doctor has to say first," Dad answers as he starts the car. Hailey falls silent for a most of the drive.

"Am I still staying with you?" Hailey asks.

"Until your mother or the courts tell me otherwise," Dad answers.

Hailey frowns. "What about Grandpa?"

"The reasons you and your mother were staying at our house are still valid," Dad answers.

Hailey nods. Dad parks in the driveway. Randy is just parking Penny's van on the street in front of the house. MaryAnn pulls up behind him. "Here are her keys." Randy tossed them at Dad. Then he gets in the car with MaryAnn and leaves.

An older woman steps out of the bushes next to the front door. "Theo, if you knew what it took to find you."

Dad frowns. "Why did you bother?"

"Now Theo, just because we had a little bit of a disagreement."

Dad snorts and then meets my eye. "Abby, run next door and see if Mrs. Vance can keep an eye on you and Hailey for an hour or so."

"I can't believe that you would call someone else in when I'm right here." The older woman starts.

I nod and run next door. Mrs. Vance agrees to come over. I go back. "She'll come."

I only hear the last part of Dad's answer. "My daughter's interests in mind or you would have stayed as far away as possible ."

"Abigail's father is gone. I think she deserves another chance."

"Abigail lost her parental rights. I will press charges if she comes within a mile of my daughter. I will bring charges against you if you tell her where we are. What I owe you is not something you want to collect."

"God says to forgive."

"I wasn't worth saving remember. If you want to save Abigail, put your own safety on the line. I want my daughter kept out of it."

The woman's mouth flaps open. Dad turns his back

on the woman and leads Hailey and me to the kitchen door.

"I'll be back as quick as I can." Dad whispers. "I won't leave until you get into the house."

Mrs. Vance comes with her big shoulder bag and ushers us into the house then turns and wave to Dad. Dad gets back in the car and drives away.

"I have cookies." Mrs. Vance leads the way to the kitchen. "How about a drink of milk and fresh cookies?"

"That sounds good." Hailey answers with her usual bubbly demeanor.

I shrug. I usually wait until supper to eat. The phone rings downstairs. "I'll get it." I rush down to the office.

"Abby Hansen, One of A Kind Designs."

"Abby, where's your Dad." Miranda Nessman snaps.

"A friend got sick and he had to go to the hospital, but I'll tell him you called when he gets back."

"Tell him he'd better have that website done if he wants any referrals out of us." A loud bang rings in my ear. I stretch out my arms to put my head on the desk and hit the keyboard. The power saver kicks out and his screen opens to where he was working when I called.

I read the lines. I know what needs to come next. Miranda's threat jumps into my head and I start typing. I don't even know how long it is just the computer and me. My eyes ache again but I ignore them.

Suddenly I am lifted out of the chair and Dad slides into the chair underneath me. "You could have said something first." I object.

"I did, you were so concentrated on the screen you haven't heard anything for hours. Mrs. Vance, she left saying like father, like daughter." Dad replies.

"I came down to answer the phone and it was Mrs. Nessman. She said to tell you that if you didn't get the website done on time what she wouldn't give you any referrals. I bumped the keyboard and your file opened and somehow I knew what to do." I try to breathe and talk at the same time, part of it is garbled.

"Take a breath, Abby." Dad instructs.

"Can you check it for mistakes?" I ask. "I don't want my mistakes to cost you more time."

"Okay." Dad looks through the lines. "I don't see anything but we can check the page in the web browser." He hit one of the F buttons along the top of the keyboard and the homepage of the website pops up. Dad goes through the pages. Everything is as I envisioned it. "It's actually an improvement over what I had in mind." Dad admits.

"So I should continue to work?"

"No, you should go up and eat supper." Dad answers. "No more computers for you today."

I slide off his lap. "Dad, how's Penny?"

"The doctors managed to help her, but then she became frantic over Hailey. I talked to the doctor and he let me bring Penny home."

Dad directs me ahead of him up the stairs. We are halfway up the stairs when the phone rings again. Dad returns to answer it while I continue up to the kitchen.

He comes up almost immediately. "Nothing important." He manages a half-smile. "I stopped off at a restaurant and ordered out dinner." He digs the stuff out of the fridge and start to fix a plate. I watch then push the plate away.

"Abby-baby, I know it's been a stressful day but you need to eat."

I look at my plate. "Could I just have a peanut butter sandwich instead?"

"You can have whatever you want." Dad gets out the

stuff for a peanut butter sandwich. Dad sets it beside me.

I pick up a triangle and take a bite. I chew and swallow. "Where's Penny."

"She and Hailey are up in her room. Abby, watch what you say. Penny lost her job today, and that's why she went into shock. I'm willing to let them stay here until she gets another one so she doesn't need to go back to her father's but she'll be very sensitive to your feelings about having her here."

"I like having Penny here." I answer.

"Okay." Dad is silent for a moment. "Sonya Snow, that lady that was here earlier, the one who called me Theo." I nod. "She might mean trouble I want you to keep an eye out for your mother and carry your cell phone every time you leave the house. You see anyone or anything suspicious the first thing you do is call me."

"Should we be leaving town?" I ask.

"We can't leave Penny and Hailey. They need us right now." Dad answers. He watches as I finish my sandwich. "I don't want you to go anywhere unless Penny or I go with you. I need you to be extra careful."

"Okay." I answer and yawn. Dad scoops me into his arms and starts upstairs. "You think you can get in your PJs and brush your teeth or are you too tired?"

"I have to brush my teeth they have peanut bugs on them." I answer. "Can I say good night to Penny and Hailey?"

"You change and brush your teeth and I'll check to see if Penny can handle saying good night." He lets me down in my bedroom.

I nod and get my pyjamas out of the drawer. I have to keep moving to stop from falling asleep. Then I go across to the bathroom to wash my face, brush my teeth, and then remember to use the toilet so then I had to wash my hands again. I come out in the hall and Dad motions me toward Penny's room.

I enter. Hailey is asleep and tucked in beside Penny. Penny is wake but she looks pale. "I came to say good night." I give her a hug.

"Abby." Her voice is very soft.

"I need you to get better soon." I glance around the room to make sure Dad stayed in the hall. "I need you to cook."

Penny frowns. "Your dad's not a bad cook."

"I'd rather have what you cook. He makes too much kd."

Penny smiles, in fact, she almost laughs. "What's nice to hear?"

"And you're the world's best Sunday school teacher." I add.

"I don't know if I can still teach Sunday School." Penny gets sad again.

"Why not?"

"People think I sinned." Tears come to her eyes. "Parents may say that I should not teach Sunday school anymore."

"More people who think Jesus isn't good enough."

Penny blink. "What?"

"Jesus says he forgives sins. If Jesus forgives you, you should be able to teach Sunday School. If these parents say that you're not good enough then Jesus' forgiveness isn't good enough for them. That's what I think."

"Out of the mouths of babes." Penny reaches out and hugs me. "Tired babies, I'll see you tomorrow."

"Good night." I stand up and almost fall over.

"Ted." Penny calls and I hear the door open.

Dad picks me up and I cuddle into his shoulder. I think I fell asleep there.

CHAPTER 11

Hailey wakes me the next morning. "Abby, get up. We have to go to computer camp. It's the last day."

I sit up. "After what happened yesterday?" I frown.

"Mom insists we paid our fees so we get to go." Hailey answers. "Come on, your dad's making pancakes."

I dress quickly and go downstairs. "Dad, are you sure you want us to go?"

"Penny insists," He speaks as he puts a plate in front of me. "I'll take you over and I'll bring her to look at your projects." Then he moves three kinds of fruit sauce within reach.

I pick the peach and spread it on my pancake. Once I finish the pancake, I go back upstairs to brush my teeth.

I come downstairs. "Dad, if you don't want me to go I'll stay home and help you with the website."

"And leave poor Hailey sitting in that class alone, that wouldn't be fair." Dad frowns. "Besides, I expect you to have my calendar finished."

I smile. "Okay."

"Penny insisted on making your lunches." Dad hands me a paper bag. "Put it in your backpack."

I go find my bag. Hailey is waiting by the door. Her eyes are shining. "Mom's all better." I am about to say something then Dad calls.

"We're waiting," I call back.

Dad comes to the door and ushers us out. We go around to the car and the strangest feeling comes over me. I look all around but I can't see anyone. "Dad?" I ask.

"I know," Dad answers, "get into the car and seatbelt yourself in."

The feeling leaves as soon as the car is moving. We get to the recreational center. Dad gets out of the car and walks us to the room. "Don't leave with anyone but me or Penny."

I nod; Hailey's eyes grow wide. "What's wrong?"

"Come on." I drag her into the room.

I sit at my computer and get immediately to work. MaryAnn stands at the front of the class. "Those of you are still working on your projects go ahead. The rest of you, we need to tidy up the classroom and decorate it for this afternoon."

I work right until noon. "Abby, are you going to get done?" Randy asks.

I stop and open the program but things just don't look right. "Something's wrong I've got to keep working," I tell Randy.

"We'll give time to you after lunch. Right now your eyes need a break." Randy answers. "In fact, I think, after everyone has eaten we're going to go out to the field and play another game of dodgeball or something. There won't be any time for an exercise break this afternoon."

It is with fresh eyes I scroll through everything until I find where the code is wrong and then rebuild the program trying to make no more mistakes while I correct the previous one. Finally, I check the final version. I think I must have said something but I don't know what. Hailey comes flying from across the room.

"What's wrong?"

"It's done, it's finally done." I smile and hold up my hand. She gives me a high five.

"Come help me, I'm putting the napkins out and making the refreshment table look inviting."

"Give me a minute to e-mail the calendar to Dad." I do that quickly before Hailey drags me along.

"I want to make a few announcements. We expect all campers to remain until three forty-five so they can discuss their project with the people we have invited. After that, you can save your project onto disk and go home when your parents are ready to leave. If the room isn't full of friends and family right at three, don't worry this is informal and we expect people to arrive anytime up to three-thirty or later." Randy raises his voice so the whole room can hear. "I want everyone to set their projects up on their computers and be ready to explain them."

I bring my calendar back up. Hailey sets up her website. Then we go back and alternate two colors of napkins and fan them out around the plates.

We just finish when a whisper goes through the room. "Three o'clock."

The door opens and five men in suits enter along with Mr. McKay. Hailey and I rush back to our seats. Randy clears his throat to get everyone's attention before he speaks. "Campers, this is Gladwin Recreational Center's board of directors. Mr. Burton, Mr. Weir, Mr. Keaton,

Mr. Anderson and the chairman of the board, Mr. Ferguson. They want to see the work that been done and hear about everything you've learned."

They start at the front when the door opens again. Penny enters. "Mom." Hailey runs to meet her. "Come see my website."

Penny hardly glances at the men as she comes to squat between our chairs. She listens to her eager daughter while Hailey shows her every page of the website.

I wait for several minutes before asking. "Where's Dad?"

"Miranda Nessman arrived late to view the website and your Dad had to stay." She pauses. "I didn't want to wait for him."

"But he will be coming?" I ask.

"As soon as he can push her out the door." Penny answers. "Show me what you've done."

"I made a personal calendar for Dad." I showed her. She laughs in all the right places. Mr. Keaton approaches us.

"Penny, I'm surprised to find you here. Your mother told me that you'd left town." He doesn't even try to smile.

"No, but as of yesterday, I'm looking for a new one." Penny answers and then takes a deep breath. "Something about lies on my application."

"Oh, no." The man turns the color of chalk. "I should have known there was something wrong when your mother answered your father's phone."

"An understatement." Penny whispers.

"I'm sorry Penny, I didn't know." He frowns. "She said you decided to move."

"I decided to stay with a friend." Penny answers.

"Oh." The man hesitates. "Come down to the plant

on Monday, I'll see what I can find."

"I don't want…"

"I've kept an eye on the work you did here. You're a good worker. Being the boss and owner, I don't have to answer to anyone for the qualifications of who I hire. Be there at eight o'clock." Penny hesitates. "Give me a chance to make it up."

"Thank you." Penny whispers.

"Least I can do." He answers and returns to the other men. Penny is shaking so I give her my chair.

"Are you alright?" I ask.

"I thought it was Dad who told him something horrible about me." Penny whispers.

"You're so nice no one would believe him." I say. Penny reaches out to hug me. I hug her back for a few seconds before letting go.

Another parent or two enters and the noise level of the room rises slightly. Randy stops by my desk. "You're looking better than you were last night."

Penny glances over at MaryAnn. "I understand I need to thank both of you for dropping off the van. Ted told me that you volunteered."

"Hey, that is what friends do." Randy answers. "Besides your two girls here put us over the minimum so the camp went ahead. We owed you. So what's the chances of getting another one together for the summer?"

"You'd have to ask either Mr. McKay or Mrs. Wilson, I don't work here anymore." Penny shrugs.

"You're joking."

"No, I was fired yesterday." Penny answers.

"Wow." Randy frowns. "Best of luck finding another job." He moves on to talk to other parents.

I look toward the door and notice that woman who called Dad, Theo, staring at me. She looks away the second I see her but I know who she is. I tug on Penny's hand.

"What Abby?"

"I need Dad." I whisper.

"What?"

"See that woman." I motion my head. "By the door."

Penny glances over. "Yes." Then she pales as a man and woman step come in behind the woman. Penny freezes.

"Penny!" I pull at her hand but she seems to go into slow motion.

Hailey stares at her mother then towards the door. She stands up. "Go away. I don't want you here." The whole room's attention suddenly focuses on the newcomers and Hailey.

"Now Hailey, is that the way you should speak to your grandmother?" The woman asks.

"It is when you hurt my mother and use your influence to get her fired." Hailey snaps back.

"Hailey!" Randy comes over. "We should not be rude to guests."

"Randy, can you call an ambulance? Penny has gone back into a shock." I pat her hand but she does not move. "Call my Dad, too."

MaryAnn immediately leaves the room and I note the woman is getting closer to me so I hang on to Penny by one hand. Hailey takes the other.

"There's no reason Hailey shouldn't meet her grandmother." The man with her grandmother answers.

"You mean other than her husband is a child molester?" The words just pop out of my mouth. There is a collective gasp in the room. I feel Penny's forehead come to rest on my shoulder as she sinks further into the chair behind her. My stomach flops into the basement.

Penny's weight leans against me and I falter a little but then lean back.

"Kimberly." The man, who had offered Penny a job earlier, speaks sharply.

"Keaton, you're taking the word of a child who isn't old enough to know what she's saying." The man accuses.

"That and my own eyes," Mr. Keaton frowns. "Since you are her mother's husband, there is no reason Penny's daughter should show a family resemblance to you."

Once people's concentration moves off me, I look around for that woman but I can't see her. I dig into my pocket for my phone. I punch out the numbers but the call is blocked by the building's concrete walls.

Mr. McKay moves to place himself in front of the man and Hailey's grandmother. "You've been asked to leave."

"I'm not going without my granddaughter. Penny obviously isn't in any condition to look after her." Kimberly sticks out her chin. "Saying such things about her step-father in the hearing of children."

"Penny is an excellent mother. " Mr. McKay corrects. "You forget I've been her boss for the last five years and upon reviewing her application, I learned that it's in someone else handwriting. Given what I've learned today, I'm willing to give her a favorable reference."

"The board will have my resignation in the morning for my part in all this, but I will say here and now that I was lied to about Penny's qualifications. What I will say is that she has done an excellent job for all that."Mr. Keaton steps back into the fray.

I am more interested in finding the woman and I turned my body to look but Penny threatens to tip so I have to push back. I glance sideways to find MaryAnn beside me.

"Abby, do you need me to make her let you go?"

"Phone Dad." I whisper.

"I did, and all I get is the answering machine." MaryAnn answers quietly.

"She's an extremely troubled young woman who's damaging her daughter with these unfounded accusations." Kimberly states.

"You've been asked to leave." Mr. McKay repeats.

Penny's stepfather steps into the fray. "I think I have a right to defend myself. I'm a minister of the gospel, not some heathen."

"Did you become that before or after you ran off with another man's wife?" Mr. Keaton asks. "Where is Roger?"

"This isn't getting us anywhere." Penny's mother tries to push past Mr. McKay. "Hailey, it's time to come home."

"My home's with Abby now." Hailey grabs onto my hand. "She's going to be my sister."

I consider contradicting her but I know I have to leave with Penny if Dad doesn't come so I keep my mouth shut. Penny's head rises from my shoulder. "I'm going to marry Ted?" I think I might have been the only one to hear the question in her voice.

"Congratulations." Mr. McKay turns to smile at Penny.

"I'll kill you both." The man rants just as the police enter through the doors behind him.

"You're under arrest for making threats." A police officer grabs one hand and starts to cuff him. The man tries to push the officer away and is soon face down on the floor.

"They have been accused of child abuse." Mr. McKay points to Kimberly and her husband. "It might take a little investigation but I think you can build a solid case."

"Who was he threatening?" The officer asks.

"Penny Whitfield and the man she's marrying, I think." Mr. McKay asks. He looks straight at me. "What's your father's name."

"Ted Hansen." I answer.

The officer looks at me. "How long ago did they come in?"

"Maybe five minutes ago."

"Everyone sit tight, we need your statements about what just happened in this room." The officer says.

Penny starts to rise. Hailey and I grab her as she slides to the floor. "I called an ambulance. She was hospitalized yesterday." Randy comes to help us get Penny back in her chair.

The ambulance arrives. Everyone is held back while Hailey and I hang on to Penny as they put her on a stretcher and take her outside. Once we are out of the building, I dial Dad's number on the cell phone.

"One of a Kind Designs, Ted-"

"Dad, Penny's on her way to the hospital again and the woman from the other day showed up at the computer camp showing." "I will meet you at the hospital." Dad says.

"Dad will meet us at the hospital," I tell Hailey. The ambulance driver allows us to ride to the hospital in the front seat with him. Hailey keeps looking back at her mom.

CHAPTER 12

We get to emergency and the nurse insists we wait outside on chairs. I keep checking every other second until I see Dad coming towards us.

"What happened?"

"My grandmother brought her husband to the show." Hailey frowns. "The police came and arrested them because they wouldn't leave. The police wanted people to stay and make statements."

Dad gives me a hug. "What about Sonya Snow?"

"The police were keeping everyone there. Only Penny went into shock again. The police let us go with her when the ambulance came."

Dad gives me another hug. "Where's Penny?"

"In there." Hailey points to a curtain. "They said for us to wait out here."

Dad nods and sits down with us.

"Dad," I pause and drop my voice, "Hailey told the police that you and Penny were going to get married so her grandparents would not be able to take her away. I just thought you should know."

"Mr. Hansen."

Dad turns. Two police officers are standing over us.

"Yes." Dad answers.

"We have some questions, Mr. Hansen."

"Can your partner sit with the girls while we can step over there to talk?" Dad indicates just down the hall.

Both officers nod. Dad gets up and goes with the officer. The second officer sits down beside us. "Could the pair of you answer some questions for me?"

I nod. Dad always says that it is better to stay on the right side of the law.

"What happened today?"

"We had the show at the computer camp. Penny came alone because Dad had a client show up and he couldn't leave right when the show started. Penny was looking at our projects when I noticed a woman who came to our house yesterday. Dad wasn't happy to have her there. I was pointing her out to Penny when two other people arrived. Those people were Penny's mother and her husband. Penny had already talked to one of the members of the board and he offered her a job to replace the one her mother got her fired from at the community center. Then Hailey told her grandmother to go away and her grandmother refused. Penny went back into shock. She ended up in the hospital yesterday after she got fired. We stuck with Penny 'cause Hailey did not want to go with her grandparents and I did not want that other woman to claim me."

"Why did you accuse Mr. Renfue?"

"Penny and Hailey came to stay with us after she found out her mother and her mother's husband were coming. The next morning Mr. Whitfield brought the pastor over and demanded Penny and Hailey move back in with him instead of staying with Dad and me. That's when I learned what happened. I knew something was really wrong because Penny had been frightened and crying since her father had told her about his visitors. Penny tried to get Mr. Whitfield to stop her mother from staying at his house but he said her mother still owned half his house."

"Which pastor?"

"Pastor Ben." I stopped and thought. "From the church over by the river."

"I think I can find him." The policeman said to me. He glances at Hailey. "Is there anything you want to say?"

Hailey frowns. "I want to stay with Abby until Mom gets better."

He frowns. "That is not my decision but I will put it in my report. Abby, do you know who that woman your Dad talked to and who showed up at your house is?"

I shake my head. "Dad said her name was Sonya something. They argued about my mother and the judge taking away her parental rights."

Dad and the other policeman come back. "We will leave you and the girls to await the doctor's verdict on Miss Whitfield." The policeman with Dad signals the officer who stayed with us to come.

"Did you answer his questions?" Dad asks.

"As best as I could." I nod.

Dad sits next to me and gives me a hug. This is followed by a long wait. Then the doctor comes out. "Mr. Hansen?"

Dad stands. "Yes."

"I am Dr. Samson. Miss Whitfield is awake. She is frantic about her daughter."

"Hailey is right here." Dad answers.

"If you could both come with us."

"How about all three of us? I don't want my daughter left here alone."

"That would be Abby?"

"Yes."

"Miss Whitfield wants to see her too." The doctor leads us into the curtained area. Penny is in bed. Her cheeks are white but she seems to gain a little color at the sight of us.

"Hailey, Abby and Ted." Penny's voice is soft.

"We were waiting for the doctor's okay to visit." Dad tells her. "Not very far away at all."

"The doctor says I can go."

"No more shocks." Dr. Samson says. "There would be no benefit in hospitalizing her but she must be kept calm."

Dad nods. "I am ready to take her home as soon as she's released."

Penny rides up front in the jalopy while we sit in the back. Dad meets my eyes in the mirror.

"Penny, I don't want to upset you, but do you have official custody of Hailey?"

"Custody?"

"Since you were a minor when she was born, there might have been a custody hearing shortly after she was born to make someone, particularly an adult, legally responsible for her. Do you remember anything like that?"

"No."

"Did you fill out the paperwork to register her birth or did someone else do it?"

Penny frowns. "I don't remember."

"Then when we get home I will call a lawyer and have

him do a search." Dad said.

The rest of the ride home is in silence.

Dad checks the house and yard before he lets the rest of us get out of the car. Once we are in the house, he walks Penny up to her bedroom and tells her to rest until supper.

"You girls go watch a movie, I have to make some phone calls before I start the meal."

Hailey and I head to the living room to put on another of her chosen four. We are ten minutes into the movie when the front door bell rings. I go look out the window then I go to the top of the stairs.

"It's MaryAnn from the computer camp." I call down.

"Coming." Dad calls so I go back to the movie. The door bell rings again but I still wait for Dad to get upstairs before anyone opens the door.

"Mr. Hansen, I brought Abby's computer disk with their projects on them." I keep one eye on the movie and one on what is happening at the door.

"What was very kind of you." Dad manages to take the disk without touching MaryAnn. "The girls will appreciate it. They are right here. Shall I call them?"

"No, that's not necessary. I just thought that, after doing the work, the girls would want to have their projects." She pauses. "I hope Penny is doing better."

"She's resting." Dad answers. "Upstairs."

"Oh, I thought she would go home since her mother and stepfather are in jail." MaryAnn steps forward.

"Not soon, if ever." Dad answers as he steps back and grasps the door handle. He starts to swing it closed. "Thank you for the disks and the concern but I have to go make supper."

"Mrs. Snow asked about Abby."

Dad stops the door in mid-swing. "And what did you tell her?"

"Nothing, it's against the recreation center policy to give out information on our students. I thought you might want to know she asked." MaryAnn moves closer to Dad and I leave the movie and go to the door.

"Hi MaryAnn, what are you doing here?" I step in front of Dad so she can't get any closer.

"I brought your calendar."

"Thank you, but you did not have to I e-mailed it to Dad when I saved it the last time."

"Oh."

"I didn't want any viruses to come home with me." I said.

MaryAnn steps back as I lean forward. "Good-bye." I say and finish shutting the door.

Dad kisses the top of my head. "Thanks, Abby-girl. I have one more phone call and then I will be up to make supper."

It seems a long time before Dad comes up to make supper. Hailey and I rip lettuce for salad. "Hailey, go call your mother for supper."

Hailey runs upstairs. Dad sits down beside me. "Abby, pack your bag, we may need to move."

"What about Penny and Hailey?"

"They have some legal things to work out."

"I take it, this Mrs. Snow is a nasty person."

"She was my foster mother before you were born." Dad answers. "Let's say that she was no friend."

"Do we have to go away permanently, can't we just go visit the dinosaurs until she goes away?"

Dad pauses. "I doubt a week's vacation is going to solve our dilemma."

"Can't you get the judge to tell Mrs. Snow to go away and leave us alone?"

"I could ask for a restraining order but that won't stop her from telling people where we are."

"Couldn't that be part of the restraining order?" I frown. "You can't build a business if we have to move every time she or someone like her finds us."

Dad sighs. "I will see what I can do, Abby-girl. Just pack that bag."

I nod. Hailey and Penny come into the room and I take my place at the table. It is a quiet supper.

CHAPTER 13

I take my books out the next morning and do a chapter of my novel study before I reach out to touch my math book. I center it in the middle of the desk and take a deep breath. I take another deep breath and open it. The sticks and arches are still there. I put my head on the desk.

"Abby, can you put a video in the machine for me?" Hailey looks at me from the doorway.

I flip the book shut and leave it where it is. The video is all picked out and waiting. Penny is sitting in the living room. I start the machine simply by pushing the video into the slot.

"Abby, come sit with us." Penny pats the couch beside her.

I sigh before I go sit down.

"What's wrong?" Penny asks.

"I can't do math," I said.

"I wish I could help you but I don't do it so well myself." Penny frowns.

I sigh again but start to watch the movie with them. I hear something. "Where's Dad?"

"Down in his office." Penny frowns. "What is it, Abby?"

"I need to talk to Dad." I jump up from my seat and head quickly to the stairs but slow down and look before I step into Dad's office. Dad's got the receiver to his ear. He nods and points to his second chair. I sit.

"I appreciate your help. I will talk to you again." He hangs up the receiver. "What is it, Abby?"

"I thought I heard something." I frown. "Maybe I'm wrong."

"Not necessarily wrong, just on alert." Dad answers. "Where are Penny and Hailey?"

"Up watching a movie."

"Why don't we go up and join them?" Dad takes the time to set the alarm on the basement door then directs me upstairs. I arrive in the living room first and sit where I was before, Dad sits on the other side of Hailey.

"What did your lawyer say?"

"He will make application for you to have full custody of Hailey in court Monday morning."

"Mr. Keaton said he would give me a job if I showed up at his business Monday at eight." Penny answers.

Dad frowns. "I don't think the custody hearing will be for a while. He is just filing papers with the courts."

Penny nods and turns her attention to the television. Dad sits back and watches. I hear the noise again and I look at Dad. He stands up and goes to the window. I hear it again and Dad sets the alarm for the front door before disappearing into the kitchen. A few minutes later he comes back and sits down.

I look at him but he just smiles and looks at the movie. The movie is nearly over when the alarm in the basement goes off. "Stay here." Dad says and goes downstairs. Penny starts to stand up but I grab her hand.

"Dad said stay here."

"Abby, what's wrong?" Penny frowns at me.

I don't say anything as the police sirens grow louder until they are parked just outside the house. My eyes stay on the stairway to the basement. Someone rings the front door bell. "Only answer it's a police officer." I tell Penny. She frowns and goes to answer it.

Police are at the front door. One of them stays there while two others take the stairs to the basement. I pray for Dad. Hailey comes and takes my hand. Penny comes back and sits with both of us.

A police officer comes back up. "How's Dad?" I ask.

"He's been knocked unconscious. You want to tell me what this is all about?"

I frown, but take him back downstairs and lead him to Dad's filing cabinet. I open a drawer and give him a file. That's when the ambulance driver and his helper arrive to put Dad on a stretcher. While the policeman reads the file I go over to see Dad, my mother stands there with her hands cuffed behind her back.

"He stole you from me. It's my time to have you." She has trouble standing steady.

"It will never be your time to have me. Dad is making a decent life for both of us and you aren't part of it and never will be."

"You're my kid." Her words are slur together.

"No, I belong to my father. The judge said so." I run back upstairs to Penny.

Penny puts her arms around me.

"Abby, what is it?"

"Can we go upstairs?" I ask.

Penny looks at the policeman at the door. He nods

and watches us go upstairs.

"Why won't you tell me what's wrong?" Penny asks.

"We need one of you that isn't in the hospital." I say.

"Abby, you have to tell me what this is about?" Penny crouches and pushes the hair out of my face.

"My mother broke the custody order. She is high. They are putting Dad in the ambulance."

"Why didn't you move this time?" Hailey asks.

I start to cry and Penny sends Hailey off to the library to read. She puts me to bed. "It's all because I couldn't do math, or we would have gone to see the dinosaurs like Dad promised. Then she wouldn't have found us."

Penny does not argue. "I will go find out how your Dad is." She kisses my forehead.

I lay there and tears pour down my cheeks for a long time and then I must have fallen asleep. I woke up, or I think I woke up but it is like my nightmare.

"Now you are going to come and take your place in the family business." The man's deep voice vibrates the window pane. He stands in front of the door, blocking my only escape with his thick arms folded across his chest.

"Where are the police?" I ask and crawl to the edge of the bed farthest away from him.

"Gone, everyone is gone, except you and me."

I scream, and I keep yelling, he comes across the bedroom and I roll into the small space between the bed and the wall then crawl under the box spring. I wait until he is stuck in between the bed and the wall I crawl out the other side and sprint for the door. I slam it shut behind me.

I see Hailey coming out of the library, I run down the hall and drag her back into the room. I close the door and drag the big chair over against it. Hailey stands there with her mouth hanging open.

"Abby!"

"Shh! So he doesn't find us." I answer as I pile the footstool in the chair seat.

I sit down on the floor with my back against the chair and pray very quietly. Hailey prays, too.

I hear lots of thumps and bumps over the next few minutes. Afterward, I hear murmurs. Finally, someone knocks on the door. "Hailey." It's Penny's voice.

I move the footstool and the chair. "Open the door." I whisper to Hailey then hide behind a bookcase.

"Mom!" Hailey says and looks beyond her mother.

"Abby's father won't allow the paramedics to take him to see a doctor unless Abby rides with him." Penny says and I can hear her frown. "Do you know where she is?"

Hailey nods. "Where are the people she is scared of?"

"The police took them away." Penny answers.

I step out and Penny grabs both our hands. She takes us right down to the basement. Dad is awake and arguing with the ambulance men. He sees me and pulls me up on his lap.

"Hailey and I will bring the car." Penny says.

Dad hands her the keys. "Watch out, who knows if those two came alone."

Penny nods. I ride the stretcher until we get into the ambulance then I get a little seat beside Dad. The driver takes his time pulling out the of the driveway and the siren is silent on the way to the hospital. Dad holds my hand with one of his and refuses to let go.

"How did you get away?"

"I crawled under the back side of the bed and waited for him to get stuck before running away." I said. "Is was just like in my nightmares, I thought of ways to get away after the last one."

"Abby-girl, I am glad you got away." Dad squeezes my hand.

I rest my head on his arm. "I am glad, too."

At the hospital, Dad does not let the nurse banish me from the examining room until he knows Penny is outside and I can sit with her. We wait for a long time before the doctor comes out.

"Miss Whitfield, Hailey and Abby."

We all nod. "Mr. Hansen is going to be fine but I want to keep him here overnight. He has a concussion." I bite my lip. "You can go visit him."

Penny takes both Hailey and me by the hand to follow the doctor back to Dad.

"I want you to go buy clothes for all three of you and then go to a hotel for the night. Come and get me before you go to church in the morning." Dad says.

"Then will you tell me what all this is about?" Penny asks.

"Yes, tomorrow afternoon. The girls can go to the park to play and we will talk." Dad answers. "Abby, hand me my pants."

I obey and Dad gives Penny some money out of his wallet.

"I can't pay you back."

"We will talk about it tomorrow." Dad says. "Right now my head hurts too much to argue."

Penny frowns but waits for me to hug my Dad before she takes my hand again. We stop at a hotel and book a room before Penny takes us out clothes shopping.

She finds us lots of clothes to try on but only lets us buy one outfit we can wear to church. Then she tries on lots of clothes and asks both Hailey and me which one we like best. She chooses one outfit for church and buys it. Then we go to a drugstore and she picks out some makeup. Then it is back to the hotel to eat supper in the restaurant before going up to the room with its two double beds.

Penny bolts and uses a lock thing on the door. We spend the evening playing with her makeup and watching the big screen television. Penny goes to bed when we do.

Dad is waiting at the hospital door when we arrive in the morning. He drives us directly to the church. Penny hesitates before getting out of the car so Dad takes her hand. He escorts her into the church and sits beside her. I sit beside Dad, and Hailey sits beside Penny.

"I have to go down and get the classroom ready." Penny speaks quickly and Dad lets her go.

Hailey moves next to me. I see Serena but she turns her head away from me. Penny comes back and sits down before the service starts. Dad puts his arm around her shoulders. When we get up to go to Sunday School, Penny stays with Dad.

Serena's mother is teaching and she asks lots of questions that have nothing to do with the Bible or Jesus. Hailey and I slip out before the class is over.

"Abby, Hailey, how was Sunday School?" Mr. Baker calls from down the hall but steps closer to hear our answer.

I pause for a second. "I don't think I will come back. Her questions about Dad and Penny were sickening. Like do they share a bedroom and do they kiss in front of us."

Mr. Baker frowns. "I will speak to her about it. You come back and there will be no such questions."

Hailey drags me away right away. "We need to find my Mom and her Dad." We go back up to the sanctuary.

We slip into the pew beside Dad and Penny. Pastor Ben frowns at us from the front of the church.

Once the service is over, Dad stands and helps Penny to her feet. He does not make out of the pew before people gather. Pastor Ben comes down to disperse those asking stupid questions while Mr. Baker clears a path for Dad and Penny to leave. Dad thanks the man before leading Penny out to the car. We all get into our seats.

"Are we going out for lunch?" Hailey asks.

"We will stop by a supermart to buy meat, cheese and buns. Then we will have a picnic in the park." Dad tells her.

I look over at Dad and Penny once in a while but I can't hear what they are saying at this distance. Hailey seems to ignore the adult conversation. She is having too much fun on the monkey bars. My cell phone rings. It never rings. I turn to Dad and he beckons me over. He takes my phone and answers it.

"Ted Hansen." I wait while he listens but I can not hear the voice on the other end of the line.

"Then we can go home. Good." He closes up the phone and hands it back.

"Can we play a little bit longer?" I ask.

"Go ahead. Penny and I have to finish talking."

I nod and run back to Hailey.

Dad calls us to the car later. Penny seems sad but Dad is his usual self. Hailey gets into the car.

"Where are we going?"

"The police tell me that it is safe to go back to the house now," Dad answers. "I want to go back and see how much cleanup I have to do in my office."

"Tomorrow is back to school." Penny glances

towards Dad. "I have to go see what job Mr. Keaton can find for me."

"You don't have to take it if it is too hard," Dad tells her.

"Yes, I do. I never finished elementary school." Penny turns her face to look out the window.

"They have upgrading classes at the community college." Dad answers.

"But no income while I do it." Penny answers.

Dad says nothing during the rest of the drive. Pastor Ben is sitting in his car outside the house when we arrive. He gets out as we pull up.

"Stay in the car a minute," Dad tells Hailey and me. I nod and wait.

"Why did he say that?" Hailey asks after Dad and Penny get out.

"He wants to talk to the pastor for a minute but he does not want us in the house until he goes in first."

"I thought the police said it was safe."

"Dad is just being extra careful," I answer. "He tends to be that way."

After a minute, Penny comes back. "Come inside."

I slip off my seatbelt and so does Hailey. We follow Penny inside and into the kitchen. She puts on the kettle. Hailey asks, "What did the pastor want?"

"To talk to Ted. They are downstairs looking at the damage to the office." Penny answers.

I watch Penny's eyes but she keeps looking away. I pause. "I need to go upstairs and do some homework."

Penny just nods. Hailey stays with Penny. I open my novel study and do the final chapter. I look at my math textbook before reaching over to open it.

The letters and number break apart and float. I try taking a dozen deep breaths but nothing helps. I sigh.

Then I close the text and go in search of Hailey and Penny.

Hailey is watching a movie about lost pets. It a classic but I watched it last week. I find Penny in the kitchen making supper.

"Need some help?" I ask.

"I would think you would want to watch the movie with Hailey." She does not look up at me.

"I watch that one all the time." I pause for a few seconds. "Penny, are you upset with me?"

Penny glances up and I see the sadness in her eyes. "Not you, just things."

"I am glad you are here. Are you sure I can't help you make the salad?"

Penny stops chopping vegetables and stares at me. "I've caused you and your Dad a lot of trouble. He almost lost the contract because of me, and you could be safely away from here."

I shake my head. "Mrs. Nessman is a difficult customer. If a kid acted that way at school, she would live in detention. The only reason Dad lets her get away with so much is her husband is a paying client. They were trying to teach her something about the creative side of business. You organizing the focus group actually helped Dad."

"What about Mrs. Snow and your mother? Your dad could have taken you somewhere safe."

I sigh. "There really is no safe place. All Dad's done is to find us somewhere to hide for a while. You helped me. She came to the computer camp but she could not get near me because you held on to me and kept me safe. Without you and Hailey, I would have spent the week alone and in even more danger. Dad was busy."

"Two trips to the hospital in two days." Penny shakes

her head. "I caused him problems."

"It got him out of his office. He needs that sometimes." I go get the lettuce and start ripping it up. "Sometimes he forgets the world exists away from the Internet."

"You think I can change that?"

I sigh, shake my head and look down at the lettuce I am ripping. "No, but you can keep me company."

Penny lifts my chin so I can see the smile in her eyes. "Thank you, Abby." I just nod and rip another piece of lettuce.

CHAPTER 14

Penny leaves before the rest of us do on Monday morning. Dad insists on driving Hailey and me to school. He stops in the office and gives the secretary his cell phone number which he promises to answer promptly. Dad warns her that I am not to leave the school alone or with anyone else except Penny. He gives her enough information about Penny for no one to make any mistakes.

I go to class. Serena looks away but I ignore her and take my seat.

Toby's voice is loud and clear to me. "Math on the board again, um, Russ. Just remember that anything divided by zero is undefined."

"Give it up Tob." Russel tells him. "Or Abigail will report you to the principal."

I take a deep breath and open my math text. Everything floats. I close it again.

"Class to your seats." Mr. Richter calls. Serena sits straight up.

"The novel study questions are due this morning." I hear gasps all over the room but I open up my book and put the written out answers in a folder. I write what it is on the label with my name and walk it up to the teacher's desk.

"Anyone else?"

The teacher asks as I sit down. The class is quiet. "I told you it was due on the twenty-sixth."

"You said we had no homework." Serena says.

"I said you had no math homework." Mr. Richter corrects. "We are going to have a test on the novel."

I sit and write the test with no problems. I am finished it early and take it to Mr. Richter's desk then I sit down. "Mr. Richter." A voice comes over the classroom P.A. System.

"Yes."

"There is a Sonya Snow here. She wishes to speak to you."

"My class is writing a test. I can not leave."

"She will be waiting at the office."

"Oh, all right I will be right there." Mr.Richter turns to the class. "I will be listening."

I open my cell phone and call home.

"Dad."

"Abby, what is it?"

"Sonya Snow is at the school and talking to my teacher right now."

"Stay where you are. I will be right there." Dad tells me.

I close the phone and wait.

Toby leans forward. "Who is Sonya Snow?"

"Abby Hansen, would you please come to the office." It is Mr. Richter's voice. I freeze in my chair.

"What's wrong, Abby?" Joe asks.

"I can't go." I say. "She's trying to take me away from my Dad."

"Is she your mother?" Toby asks

"No." I shake my head.

"Abby Hansen, to the office please."

"Mr. Richter is going to be mad." Serena tells me.

"Just because you have a crush on the teacher does not mean I shouldn't wait for Dad to get here." I tell her.

Serena turns red. A few of the students snicker.

I ignore her and go to the window to look out at the parking lot.

"Abigail Hansen, to the office!"

I see Dad's car pull into the parking lot and take a breath.

"Abigail, I told you to come to the office." Mr. Richter is in the doorway.

"There is no Abigail in this class. My name is Abby and my father told me not to go nowhere with anyone but him." I answer.

"Mrs. Snow is from child protection services."

"Mrs. Snow is a liar." I tell him. "Call child protection services and ask."

Mr. Richter comes and grabs my arm.

"Let go of my daughter." Mr. Richter turns to see Dad in the doorway.

"She is going to child protection services. She has been kidnapped from her mother."

Dad grabs Mr. Richter by the collar and the arm. Dad squeezes until Mr. Richter lets go of me. Dad twists Mr. Richter's arm behind his back so he faces the blackboard. "Sonya Snow is a kidnapper and you are aiding and abetting. Abby, get your things, you are not going back here."

I go to my desk and take out everything. I leave the

textbooks on the seat then I get my gym strip and my backpack. I stuff everything into my backpack.

"Time to go, Abby-girl."

"You will go to jail for this." Mr. Richter tells Dad.

"Theo." Mrs. Snow arrives at the door not five feet from Dad.

Dad reaches out and grabs Sonya Snow. "Abby, go to the office and have Ms. Shelby call the police."

I run to the office and tell the secretary what is happening. She calls nine-one-one.

I stay at the office until the police come. Dad has to follow the police car to the station so we can make statements.

"Abby, I think we have to leave." Dad says as he waits for the office to finish typing out papers for Dad to sign.

"We can't go without saying goodbye to Penny and Hailey." I frown.

Dad glances at the policeman. "I will try to reach Penny."

I hand him my phone. Dad has to ask the police officer for the phone directory. The man tells Dad to use his desk. I sit and wait in a nearby chair.

"I had to leave a message." Dad tells me when he comes back to sit beside me.

"What about your business?"

Dad shakes his head. "I sent backup files to the remote server. The filing cabinets can be shipped."

"Who is going to keep Hailey and Penny safe now?"

"Abby, you are my first concern."

"Where are we going this time?"

"Nowhere until Penny calls."

My phone rings. Dad goes and picks it up. He listens

for a minute. "Penny, calm down." "Take some deep breaths so I can understand you." "I need you to come down to the police station to sit with Abby." "I will deal with the rest of it. Just come."

"What?" One of the policemen asks.

"Hailey's grandfather took her out of school this morning without her mother's permission. I have to go talk to the man."

"I will come with you." The officer tells him. "My partner can stay with Abby."

"Abby, watch for Penny. She's upset."

I nod. Dad and the policeman leave.

It takes about five minutes for Penny to arrive and the policeman has me identify her before he allows her to sit with me.

"Penny." I hug her and lead her to a chair.

"Your Dad's message said you have to leave."

"Not before Dad talks to you. He promised."

"But you have to leave."

"Mrs. Sonya Snow came to the school and lied to my teacher about being from child protections services. Mr. Richter was going to let her take me. I phoned Dad. The police were called. That's why we are here."

Penny frowns. "Where is your Dad?"

"Dad and a policeman went to talk to Mr. Whitfield about Hailey."

"Dad is Hailey's guardian. The school had to let him take her." Tears start rolling down Penny's cheeks. "I have no legal rights."

"Dad has his lawyer working on it."

"There isn't enough time to change things." Her keys fall from her fingers and land on the floor by the chair.

I could see Penny slipping backward. I ask the policeman to bring me a glass of cold water. I hold for her to sip it and spill it down her blouse.

"Sorry."

Penny looks at herself and starts to cry. I give her a hug. "Dad will help."

"There is no help."

The phone rings. The policeman picks it up. "Miss Whitfield is right here."

I wait for Penny pick up the phone. "Mr. Keaton. I am sorry. It's hard to explain. Dad took Hailey from school without my permission." "I don't know where Mom and her husband are." "Thank you for understanding." "I will call."

Penny hangs up the phone and sits back on the chair.

I come and sit down next to her. "I am sorry about spilling water on you."

"You kept me from going back into shock. I am not very strong."

"Maybe you and Hailey could come with us."

"My father could charge us with kidnapping for taking Hailey away."

I fall silent. There does not seem to be anything to say.

"I guess I have to go back to my father's house." Penny rises.

"Talk to my Dad first. He promised to speak to you before we leave."

"I have to be with Hailey. Your dad won't let anything happen to you. I can't let anything happen to Hailey." Penny answers. "I have to go pack our things."

"You can't go there until the police say it's safe. They don't know how many people my grandfather has working for him. I need you to stay until Dad comes back."

Penny pauses. She looks at me then at her shirt. "I

need to go to the bathroom and clean up."

The man shows Penny the way to the washroom.

I phone Dad.

"Dad."

"What is it, Abby?"

"Have you got Hailey yet?"

"It is a little more complicated than that," Dad says.

"Penny thinks she has to go back to her father's to protect Hailey. She's in the washroom right now. How do I keep her here?"

"You can't, she's an adult."

"Penny almost went back into shock just thinking about us leaving. Who is going to look after Hailey once Penny ends up in the hospital?"

"Abby- slow down, I am not finished but I have to figure out something that Mr. Whitfield wants."

"Other than the jalopy?" I ask.

"Probably."

"His house," I sigh. "He was more worried about that people said than about Penny."

"Thanks, Abby. I will be there as soon as I can."

I close the phone. It only seems like a moment later when Penny comes back. "Sorry Abby, I have to go find Hailey. The policeman will watch you until your Dad comes."

Penny reaches into her pockets then searches her purse. "Where are my keys?"

I pause then say. "You dropped them when you sat down."

Penny looks at the floor.

The police officer comes over. "I am sorry Miss Whitfield, but I need your statement about what has been going on."

Penny sighs. She goes over to sit at the policeman's

desk where I can see her. He seems to ask a lot of questions. Penny answers them but her cheeks get very pale. I almost cry out a warning before he lets her come back and sit beside me. She seems shaky. "He says I have to stay."

My phone rings. I answer it. "Abby."
"Yes, Dad." I look up at Penny.
"Is Penny there?"
"She's right here."
"Can I talk to her?" I hand Penny the phone.
"Ted." She listens for a while. "The policeman downstairs won't let me leave the station house."
"Okay, we will wait for you."
I take a deep breath.

We leave the station in Dad's car. We go to the courthouse. Hailey and her grandfather were waiting for us.

Dad's lawyer shows up and takes us in to see the judge. The judge listens to everything. Mr. Whitfield signs over Hailey's custody to Penny but only after the judge marries Dad and Penny.

I ask after the lawyer and Mr. Whitfield leave. "Do we still have to leave?"

"We do, but Penny and Hailey are coming with us," Dad tells me.

Penny frowns. "Where are we going?"

"I usually don't make that decision until I am on the road." Dad pauses. "Let's get away from where we can be overheard and discuss it."

CHAPTER 15

We wind up back at the park, but this time, Dad and Penny walk over to the monkey bars so we are closer in case anything happens. Dad and Penny talk for a long time. I climb for a bit then sit on the top of the monkey bars and look around before going back to climbing with Hailey. I do this a few times before Dad calls us down.

"Time to go."

Dad drives to the airport and parks in long term parking. Dad buys tickets and we board a plane. Hailey stares at everything. I give her the window seat so she can see outside. Dad and Penny sit behind us.

"What about our stuff?" Hailey asks me.

"Dad will take care of it," I say.

Hailey frowns but turns to stare out the window.

After we land Dad rents a car and we go clothes shopping before we find a hotel for the night. The next morning we end up driving for hours and all the scenery is just flat grassland. All of a sudden the road goes down and we are going down into desert canyons. Then there are houses but Dad does not stop until we arrive at a large building with a gigantic T-Rex in front.

I read the sign on the outside of the building the Royal Tyrrell Museum. "But I messed up my math."

"Penny and I need some time to discuss where we are going to live. It was Miranda Nessman's demand for a new website and not your math that changed our plans last week." Dad tells me as we get out of the car. "Have fun, Abby."

I grab Hailey and run to the door but we have to wait for Dad and Penny to pay our way inside. Dad tells us to keep in sight. Hailey is interested in everything but I want to listen to the sounds that the scientists think the dinosaurs made. The skeletons reach so high that we have to go to a second floor to see the heads up close.

Still occasionally I look back to see how Dad and Penny are doing. Often they are standing or sitting talking but I am rarely near enough to hear what they are saying. At the end of the day, Dad takes us to a hotel for the night.

We stay for five whole days before Dad and I end up walking together because Hailey wants to show Penny something in the gift shop.

"Where are we moving?" I ask.

"Penny does not want to move anywhere. She wants to take the job Mr. Keaton offered her."

"Can we move back without being found?" I ask.

Dad pauses in front of an exhibit of a hadrosaur. "It depends on if the police manage to keep your grandfather, Mrs. Snow and your mother in custody. We could still be in trouble if they are granted bail or get short sentences."

I sigh. "What about Hailey's grandmother and her husband?"

"Penny thinks that they will leave her alone now that the judge has given her custody."

I frown. "That never stopped mom and grandfather."

"Penny does not want to depend on me for things. I want her to go to school to qualify for a better job, but that would mean not earning any money for a while and she thinks she needs to pay her own way."

"Is she scared to go back to school? She said that math was too hard so she could not help me with mine."

"She might be." Dad runs his fingers through his hair.

"You could teach her how to set up web pages." I pause. "She worked in the office at the community center. Maybe you wouldn't have to work so many hours if you had help."

"Those are good ideas but I think she wants to try working for Mr. Keaton first."

I study the ferns the hadrosaur is eating. "Then you have to let her. She is an adult."

Dad puts his hand on my shoulder. "I guess I need to remember that."

"Dad, Penny and Hailey are staying with us?"

"I am trying to convince Penny to stay."

I think for a few minutes. "The best way might be to let her try things her way but tell her that we need her. I mean if we are not going to move then you need someone to help keep an eye on me. And someone needs to watch Hailey in case her grandmother comes back."

"I will talk to her again." Dad tells me.

On the seventh day, Dad announces that we are going home. We pack up the car and drive back to the airport. Dad buys tickets and we fly back only Dad sits next to

Hailey while Penny sits next to me.

Penny is silent most of the way home. Dad is talking to Hailey about where she should try to publish her writing.

"Abby, you have to convince your Dad to move away so you are safe." Penny speaks quietly when Dad and Hailey seem absorbed in their conversation.

"Why did you marry my Dad?"

Penny sighs. "Your Dad married me because my father insisted on it."

"Dad married you because he cares about what happens to you. Nothing Mr.Whitfield did would have made Dad do anything if he hated the idea. Nothing Mrs.Snow did, changed his mind about my mother."

There is a long pause.

"Abby, you have to convince him."

"I don't want to convince him, I like you and Hailey too much. If you want us to move away, then you have to come with us."

The house is quiet when we get home. We each take our suitcases upstairs and unpack. When I come down Penny is cooking supper and Dad is downstairs rearranging his office. Hailey is watching a movie. I go down to the office.

"Have you listened to the messages?" I ask.

"Why?"

"The school might have phoned."

Dad reaches over and presses the button on the phone. "You have ten new messages.

First message. Bill Nessman here.Ted call me when you get back to business. I have a friend who wants a teen website for a skateboard start up.

Second message. This is Miranda Nessman. I want

some changes to the website.

Third message. Theo, they tell me that Abigail and her father are expected to go to jail. You-" Dad punches the button to skip the rest of message.

"Fourth message. Pastor Ben here. I want to speak to Ted and Penny. Marriage is a big step, and although it's too late for premarital counseling I am willing to offer what assistance I can to help with your adjustment to married.

Fifth message. Ted, I need a website. Call me and we'll talk.

Sixth message. Mr. Hansen, this is Madge at Grissom Financial." Dad hits the skip button again.

"Seventh message. Penny, Hailey is my granddaughter. Your father must have lost his mind giving you custody. My lawyer will be calling.

Eighth message. Mr. Hansen, this is Mrs. Shelby. I need to speak to you about Abby's unexplained lengthy absence. Call during school hours. Ninth message. This is Mr. Richter, Abby's teacher. She is missing far too much school. I have called in child protection.

Tenth message. Mr. Hansen, this is Betty Carter at child protection we have spoken to police and reviewed the file. Please understand that we need to check up on Abby. If you can, call me during business hours."

"Are you going to call?"

"Tomorrow morning." Dad answers. "It is after regular hours now."

"Can I change schools?"

"It might be a good idea. You and Hailey should be in the same school."

I nod and go upstairs. I skip the living room and go to the kitchen. Penny is still cooking so I set the table. Dad comes up in a short while and makes the salad. He nods at me so I go watch the end of the show with Hailey.

Dad calls us for supper but Penny looks upset. Hailey frowns at her mother then at Dad.

"Hailey," Penny starts. "Ted wants Abby to transfer to your school. We need to you to keep an eye out for one another."

"Is that why you are upset?"

"No, your grandmother left a message for me on the answering machine. We have to be careful until she and her husband leave town."

Hailey takes a deep breath and sighs. "I told them to go away."

"It seems that they are not good listeners." Dad says.

"I have to phone Mr. Keaton." Penny leaves her meal uneaten.

Dad phones child protection early the next morning. He asks for Betty Carter by name. It is a short conversation and she shows up just after breakfast. She talks to Hailey and me. Hailey asks her about getting protection from her grandmother. The woman explains custody to Hailey. I answer her questions about Dad and how we went to see the dinosaurs. She shakes hands with both Dad and Penny before she leaves. "I wish all children were in such good hands."

Dad takes Hailey to school before we go visit Mrs. Shelby at my old school. Dad signs papers at the office before taking me back to Hailey's school and registering me into class.

I am a grade ahead of Hailey so we are not in the same classroom. I find her at recess.

"Hailey." I see her out on the field playing kickball with some other students.

She runs back to me. "Abby, I thought your dad must

have changed his mind."

"No, I ended up in Mrs. Gates' class." I answer as we go out to the field.

"You must have a birthday near the beginning of the year."

"March."

"Hey, Hailey, who's the new kid?" One of the kickball players calls.

"This is Abby, she's my new sister." Hailey calls back.

All the kids come over to meet me. I try to remember names but there are too many to keep in my head. We spend the rest of recess playing kickball.

I go back to class and the teacher hands me a math text. I take a deep breath and open it to the page she tells me. It is not word problems and the numbers are easy to read. I take another deep breath and get to work.

Dad shows up at the end of the day to drive Hailey and me home. "Come downstairs, I looked up some e-zines that accept children's writing. Abby, you come join us and tell me how your first day of the new school went."

"I ended up in Mrs. Gates class. She has us sit in groups and lets us talk about our assignment. It's a lot different than Mr. Richter's class." I watch as Dad directs Hailey to sit in his second chair. He brings up a list of websites that take kid's writing. A few of them have writing contests.

Hailey gets really excited about all the sites as Dad shows them to her. I smile as I watch her.

We hear Penny come home. Hailey runs upstairs to greet her. "Ted." Hailey calls.

Dad goes upstairs. They are taking a long time so I go up to see what is happening.

Hailey is sitting in the kitchen.

"Where is she?"

"Your Dad took her upstairs. He said he would come down and cook supper in a little while."

"We might as well watch a movie. Dad only lets me go on the internet when he can watch." I tell her. She follows me into the living room. "We might have to move."

I frown. "Why?"

"I don't think Mom is going to keep her new job. Then we won't be able to pay your Dad rent."

"You and your mom don't have to pay rent to live here." I frown.

Hailey starts to say something then closes her mouth. She sighs. She perks up a little when I let her pick the movie.

Dad calls us for supper but Penny is not at the table. "Penny is lying down. Her new job is very hard."

Penny is limping the next morning but she goes off to work before Dad drives Hailey and me to school. Mrs. Gates is a kind lady who takes the time to go over what the class has already covered in each subject. At recess and lunch hour, I play with Hailey and her friends. Dad comes to pick us up.

"Penny came home early. She's resting so I want you to find something quiet to do so she can sleep." Dad tells Hailey and me.

Penny gets up for supper. She moves very slowly and closes her eyes whenever a noise is too loud.

"Ted, I think I have to quit."

"Okay." Dad says.

Tears spring into her eyes. "We will find somewhere else to live."

"With what money?" Dad asks.

Penny sighs and leans on her hands. "We can not live off you."

"Penny, what did you do at the community center?" Dad asks.

"I set up training programs like the computer camp."

"And how did you do that?"

"I kept a list of subjects people asked about classes in. I found instructors. Then I made a list of those who registered interest by filling out a form. I organized classroom space and choose the best time for the majority of the people. I phoned everyone to see if they wanted to register. I got everyone signed up. Then when the class started, I made sure that the instructors had everything they needed, and was on hand if there were any problems."

"Did you do any filing?"

"Yes, I kept the paperwork straight."

"Would you get upset if I offered you a job?"

"Doing what?"

"Keeping my office in order so I can be more efficient building websites," Dad answers. "Instead of participants, we have clients. Instead of courses, we have websites. And instead of instructors, you have me. Mostly there is a pile of paperwork that needs organizing and filing. And someone to answer the telephone so it does not interrupt my programming."

"I don't know anything about websites."

"I handle the creative stuff, you get stuck with the paperwork and answering the phone. If you want to learn, I will let you look over my shoulder. Ten dollars an hour to start."

"I have trouble with numbers." Penny admits.

"My accounting gets e-mailed to a bookkeeper. I make more money per hours doing websites than I pay her to do the books. It's keeping separate files for each site so I know where to look to find the information that I would like you to organize."

"Is this a sympathy position?"

"No. With some help organizing the files, there should be fewer weeks when I have to work around the clock."

"But ten dollars an hour?" Penny frowns.

"It is what he paid Roland for tutoring me in math." I say.

"Then you can run errands for me when I do have a significant project due so Abby and Hailey are not reducing to cheese, tuna, and peanut butter sandwiches for days on end."

Hailey asks. "Can we still live here?"

"You can continue to live here whether your mom takes the job or not." Dad tells her. "You and your mom are part of my family now."

Hailey glances at her mother. "Really!"

"You can even put your books in the library so you never have to give one away again." I tell her. "You can even choose which shelf to put them on."

Penny glances at her daughter. Light comes into Hailey's eyes. Penny pauses. "On trial. In case, you don't like my work."

CHAPTER 16

We write a test in math of Friday. I get 92 percent right. The teacher says that we have to take the test papers home and get our parents to sign them. I put it in my backpack.

I get home and leave the test paper beside Dad's place at the table. I follow Hailey downstairs, Penny is putting papers in files. Dad is sitting at his computer. Hailey takes the second chair so she can use the second computer to see if any of the e-zines has accepted her writing. I glance around then I go upstairs to do my history homework.

Penny comes up to my room. "What are you doing?"

"My homework."

"Did you want time on the computer?"

I shake my head. "I have all the answers I need in my textbook."

"What are you studying?"

"History." I answer. "I just have a few questions to do. I will come down and help with supper when I am done."

Penny nods. "Okay."

I come down and rip up lettuce for salad and set the table. Dad and Hailey come up when Penny calls them. Dad looks at the test. "What's this?"

"The teacher said I had to bring it home and get it signed." I say.

Dad looks through the pages. "No trouble with this math." He reaches for a pen off the pad near the phone and signs the paper. He hands back the paper. I sit on it until after supper is over.

Pastor Ben comes after supper and talks with Dad and Penny downstairs. I take the test back upstairs to put in my backpack. Hailey comes to my room and we make bead bracelets. It is lots more fun with Hailey than it ever was alone.

Dad comes up to tuck me into bed. "Good job on the math test."

I nod. "It was all numbers and no word problems."

"You will tell me if you have any trouble when you have to do a word problem." Dad says.

I answer. "I promise."

"Good, now get some sleep." He kisses me on the forehead.

"Dad, why is Penny scared I will get upset if you spend time with Hailey?"

There is a short silence. "Penny is not used to anyone helping her without getting something back. She does not understand what we get from having her and Hailey here."

I sigh. "Why doesn't she get that we need her here?"

This time, there is a longer silence. "Because she thinks we pity her." Dad finally answers. "We just have to keep showing her how much we need her and hope she adjusts."

I nod. Dad kisses my forehead again. "Good night, Abby."

Saturday Dad takes the day off and we go to the park for part of it but instead of climbing on the monkey bars he brings a soccer ball for us to kick around. Hailey has fun but Penny seems thoughtful and withdrawn.

I try to keep her in the game by passing the ball to her so she can not sit down. I am afraid that she is going to feel left out. When Penny lets the ball go, Dad sends Hailey and me off to the monkey bars so he can talk to Penny.

Hailey climbs the monkey bars but keeps glancing back at Dad and Penny. "Why is your Dad holding Mom's hand?"

"He's her husband. Husbands and wives hold hands in the movies." I tell Hailey. Although I really think it is the only way he can keep her still enough to hold a conversation.

"Oh." Hailey thinks about this for a while. "In the movies, husbands and wives share bedrooms."

"Except your grandfather pushed them to get married, Dad is not going to make Penny do things she isn't ready to do."

Hailey glances at me. "Grandfather said that that is all men want from women."

I want to tell her that her grandfather is not always right but I doubt she will believe me. "Dad likes Penny and he wants her to stay. He is not going to hurt her."

Hailey frowns. "But-"

"But nothing, we want both of you to stay. Dad is doing his best to calm Penny down. He knows how upset she gets over things. He does not want her to end up in the hospital." I frown and climb to the top of the bars so I can look around.

Hailey climbs slower but she makes it to the top of the bars. "Abby, are you mad at me?"

"Dad has been nice to you and helped you to find a place to publish your writing. You still accuse him of trying to hurt your Mom." I start to climb down.

Following me down Hailey pauses. "Some men have tried to get to Mom by being kind to me."

I sigh but say nothing more for a few minutes finally I have to add. "It is fun having a sister to hang out with, and I like Penny. Before you came, it was just Dad and me. Dad works long hours so I spent a lot of time alone. Why can't you just believe that Dad just wants company and what is best for you and Penny?"

Hailey sighs. "Grandfather made Penny pay rent and buy groceries. He only listened if I went out and talked while he worked on other people's cars for free. It's hard to believe people are as nice as your Dad without them wanting something."

"You can pay him back by being happy. He needs cheerful people around him." I tell her.

Hailey pauses for a minute but she does not get a chance to speak before Dad calls us to the car.

Penny seems nervous for the rest of the day. Dad makes supper and we all watch a movie before he sends Hailey and me up to bed. Dad comes up to tuck me in.

"How was your talk with Hailey?" Dad asks.

I should have known he was watching.

"Hailey listens to her grandfather too much." I sigh. "She thinks you are going to hurt Penny."

"Hurt Penny how?"

"She said her grandfather told her that men only want

one thing from women."

"I see." Dad sits back on the edge of the bed.

"I tried to tell her that you don't want Penny back in the hospital."

"You think I should talk to Hailey?"

"I think you should talk to Penny." I say.

"I've tried talking to Penny." Dad tells me. "Convincing her is more difficult."

"Maybe you and Penny should talk to a counselor." I frown. "Then you can understand her. What she expects being married to be like."

"Expects?"

"Before I changed schools, I expected teachers to be just like Mr. Ritcher, but Mrs. Gates does things her own way. He expected everyone to sit quietly and work without talking. Mrs. Gates like us to work on projects together and she wants us to talk about what we are doing with the other students in our group.

Before Penny lived with her father and he expected her to pay rent and buy groceries. Hailey said that she had to go out to the garage and talk while he worked to get him to listen. Once you get really working you don't like anyone to talk to you. You prefer to spend time with me separate from your job. I know you don't expect me to pay rent or groceries. You don't even like me to do housework and Penny did all the housework. So maybe you need to find out what would make Penny happy instead of thinking she can change to suit you."

Dad pauses. "You think your old dad can change?"

"If you want Penny to stay then you have to try." I pause and then hug Dad. "I love you but the house will seem empty if they leave."

"I know it will, Abby-girl." He hugs me back then kisses my forehead. "You go to sleep and I will go listen to Penny."

I nod and yawn. He pulls the covers up to my shoulders.

The next morning is Sunday so we go to church. Penny is back to teaching Sunday School. Serena sits on the other side of the group. Hailey and I ignore her for the most part. Penny continues with how Jesus deals with people in the New Testament. We answer the questions on the paper from weeks ago in a discussion because no one remembers to bring the papers back.

"Miss Whitfield." Serena starts to ask.

"Mrs. Hansen." I say.

"What?" Serena looks at me for the first time.

"Her name is Mrs. Hansen." I answer. "She married my Dad."

"What was your comment, Serena?" Penny asks.

"How come you did not get married in the church?" Serena asks.

"That is not part of the Sunday School lesson, we were talking about Jesus healing the blind man. Does anyone have a comment or question about that?" Penny asks.

I put up my hand. "What did Jesus get out of healing the blind man?"

"Now that is an excellent question." Penny says. "Jesus wanted to help people because God told him to show God's love to men so they would glorify God. Healing was something that people recognized as coming from God because they could not heal themselves."

I nod. "Then what do we get from helping each other?"

"We get pleasant feelings, sometimes we get praise, and sometimes if we tell people, it is because of Jesus we get them to thank God." Penny answers. "If we do it for Jesus it is to get people to praise God."

The rest of the lesson is about getting people to praise God for what he has done.

Sunday afternoon, Dad takes us down to an art gallery to look at the pictures while he talks to an artist who wants a website. The man who owns the art gallery is a client of Dad's and he sends artists who want an original site to show off their art to Dad. We are only part way through the gallery when Dad calls us over to him.

Dad puts Penny between him and the artist. Dad keeps his arm on Penny's shoulders. "Bertie, this is my wife, Penny, and our daughters, Abby, and Hailey. Penny, this is Bertie Babbity. He creates mobiles."

"I prefer to call them bobbing bobbles." Bertie makes an exaggerated gesture with his hands and arms.

"Penny is also my office assistant," Dad says. "You will be dealing with her on a regular basis."

The man ignores this and looks at Dad. "When we will meet again."

"Actually, I would prefer if you would e-mail me pictures of your work. Professionally done pictures to show the works to their best advantage. Since you have firm ideas of what you want, I think I can do up a mockup or two. I will send you a server link so you can view the results and comment on them by e-mail before you decide on the final design." Dad tells him.

Hailey gives me a look but any explanation has to be left until we get away from the gallery. Penny seems fine with Dad's touching her.

"Then everything is set." The gallery owner comes over. "Ah, the lovely new Mrs. Hansen. Where I thought, Ted was destined to spend his life alone in that cave he calls an office." He kisses Penny's cheek.

Penny blushes. Hailey rolls her eyes. Dad slips his arm from Penny's shoulders to her waist and tugs her a little closer.

Bertie Babbity draws out a sigh. "Yes, new love, isn't it splendid."

I know he does not mean it. I also know enough to keep quiet while Dad handles business.

"Abby, did you see the new dinosaur pictures by Mrs. Gold?" The gallery owner asks.

"No, we didn't get that far," I answer.

"Then come along. Bertie has a showing across town tonight and we don't want to keep him." The man directs Dad, Penny, Hailey and me across the gallery leaving Mr. Babbity to clean up his mobiles and go.

Mrs. Gold's pictures looked only a little like the dinosaurs in the museum. She uses different colors and adds skin flaps so they almost look like dragons but not quite. Dad will never buy one because he said that I have enough nightmares without waking up to see one of Mrs. Gold's paintings looking down at me.

Dad takes us out to supper at a sit-down restaurant. Penny's expression say she wants to object.

"Working on that man's stuff is going to be a headache." Dad seats Penny and tries to change the subject.

"Why?" Hailey asks.

"He and I have very different ideas about business relationships," Dad answers. "So long as most of our communication can be done over the Internet I can deal with him."

I say nothing but order a meal that Dad never cooks. Hailey orders the same meal as me but that doesn't bother me. Penny looks like she wants to cry. Dad starts to discuss the options with her as if he is still making up his mind. The waitress answers Dad's questions until Penny picks something then orders the steak I knew he would.

Penny starts to relax after the server leaves as Dad includes the three of us in a discussion about what to do the next weekend.

"Abby, what do you think we should do?" Penny asks.

I consider my answer for a few minutes. "Since you didn't get to invite people to the wedding, I think we should have a party to celebrate."

Penny glances down to the table.

"Next weekend does not give us enough time to send out invitations and give people enough time to plan to come." Dad shakes his head. "We need at least six weeks to plan anything like that."

"Ted?" Penny glances up at him.

"I am not ashamed to be married to you. I say we have good reason to have a party." Dad tells her. "I just think it takes more than a week to plan such an event."

The waitress returns with our plates. It takes a moment before she leaves and Dad asks Hailey to pray.

"We could even invite the pastor to come and bless the marriage." I say once we are eating.

Dad winks at me.

Penny looks a little stunned but Hailey smiles. "We could invite all our friends."

"We have to give Penny a little while to get used to the idea. She might have some ideas of her own." Dad smiles at both of us.

CHAPTER 17

I feel good about what's happening until I get into math the next day and Mrs.Gates announces we are going to do word problems. I open the text and shake my head. I go to the front of the room to talk to the teacher.

"What is it, Abby?"

"I have trouble with word problems." I say.

"Many students do." She smiles and signals for me to pull a chair up to her desk. "You are good in math otherwise, so what is your difficulty with word problems."

I sit. "I had to do a word problem on the board in front of the class I was in before this one. Some boys were teasing me and I got real upset. Now when I try to read a problem the words and numbers break apart and float around on the page like little sticks and arcs."

"You can read words and numbers at other times."

I nod. "It's just word problems."

Mrs. Gates picks up the textbook. "Do the questions on page 124 instead. I will talk to the learning assistance teacher today and see if she knows how to deal with your problem."

I go back to my desk. Page 124 is just numbers, and I finish it in class.

After school, I go downstairs with Hailey but I go over and hug Dad. "What's up, Abby?"

"We started word problems today." I say. "I still can't read them. I explained the problem to the teacher and she said she would ask the learning assistance teacher."

"If they can't help you then I will find a counselor for you."

I nod. "I have some science homework to do." I go upstairs to my room.

I work for a while then go downstairs to help Penny with supper. I set the table and make the salad.

Penny watches me. "What did you talk to your Dad about?"

"Word problems in math." I say. "Do you want me to put anything else in the salad?"

"No."

I nod and start to leave. "Abby, why did you suggest the party on Sunday?"

"Serena's comments in Sunday School. I want people to know I have a new mom."

"You and your dad didn't talk about it before Sunday night?"

"I hadn't thought about it until Sunday."

Penny pauses. "Do you really want to tell the world that your Dad and I got married?"

"I want you to be happy that you and Dad are married. Dad thinks it's worth celebrating and so do I."

"But-"

"I can't make the past go away. I want you and Hailey

to stay so Dad has a reason not to work all the time. I know he has problems with allowing people to get close to him but he tries with you and Hailey. Can't you quit worrying about money long enough to realize that Jesus said that it wasn't the most important thing. The most important thing is to help each other. You help Dad by being here."

"You really think so."

"He never trusted anyone to help in the office before even though he's needed assistance for years."

Penny blinks. "Ted trusts me." She turns back to her cooking. She stirs the spaghetti sauce.

The learning assistance teacher, Miss Franklin, comes to our class at math time the next day. She has gray hair, but she wears neat clothes. I think I have seen her at church. She takes me back to her classroom.

"Now Abby, what happened?"

I explain what happened and how I could not read certain questions in my math textbook. "Your problem is not so much about math as it is about being upset. Somehow you have to break the link between math problems and being in emotional distress."

"How do I do that?" I ask.

"Let's try this." She opens a copy of my textbook to word problems.

I look at the page but it's just a bunch of floating sticks. I shake my head.

"How do you feel, Abby?"

Concentrating on my feelings, I say. "Upset."

"I want you to take a deep breath and try to relax."

I follow her instructions but the sticks still float.

"Another deep breath."

Again I take a deep breath. Nothing changes. I shake

my head.

"I can send a note to the school psychologist asking for help." Miss Franklin says. "It might take a little while. You can go back to class now."

Dad and Penny start planning their reception. Dad does up some invitations on the computer and Penny is addressing the ones that can not be sent out by e-mail.

"Next weekend, we are going clothes shopping so everyone has new clothes for the party." Dad tells me.

I come for a hug. "What's wrong, Abby?" Dad asks.

"The learning assistance teacher is calling the school psychologist," I say. "It's going to take some time."

Dad nods and kisses my forehead. I hug him back. "I am going upstairs to read."

I wind up just staring at the ceiling. There is a book in my hands but I am not actually reading. Hailey comes to find me.

"We get new clothes."

"It should be fun." I say because I know she's excited.

"Abby, what's wrong?"

"Just trouble with math," I answer.

"Neither Mom nor I am any good at math."

"It's not really math." I pause because this is hard to explain. "I get upset when I see one kind of math question because I was teased in front of the whole class at my last school."

"I get upset whenever I see any kind of math questions 'cause I never know where to start."

"Do you have your math books here?"

Hailey shakes her head. "There's no point bringing it home Mom can't help me and neither would my grandfather."

"Bring it home tomorrow if I can't help you then Dad can."

Hailey nods.

Hailey brings her math home. Dad has us do it downstairs so if we need help, he is right there. All the stacks of paper are filed so Penny is busy planning the party. She is surrounded by lists.

"If all these people come we will have no room to move in here." Penny frowns.

Dad goes to the computer and brings up his accounts. "I have some money in the entertainment account. Rent the community center if necessary."

"What?"

"If you think we need a bigger space rent it."

"The invitations have been sent. We can't change the location now." Penny frowns.

Dad stops. "You are right. We could rent a tent for the backyard if there are too many people for the house."

"What would that cost?"

Dad turns to his second computer to boot up the Internet to find a rental company. He waves Penny over and seats her in his second chair. "Come and pick out what we need."

Penny looks at the screen. "That's a lot of money."

"Ignore the prices for a minute, what size of tent or tents do you think we need?"

"I don't want to go into debt." Penny frowns.

"We won't, I have some cash tucked away but no credit cards. I will tell you if you come anywhere close to spending it."

"You promise not to go into debt over this party?"

"I promise." Dad answers. "Just pick out what we need."

Dad and Penny get into a discussion over that kind of tent. Hailey and I work on her math until the phone rings. Penny answers it then gives it to Dad.

"Who is it?"

"Bertie Babbity."

"This may take some time."

Penny goes upstairs to make supper.

"Time to go watch a movie until supper." I tell Hailey. "We can work on this later."

Hailey gathers her books and takes them upstairs. She comes down to the living room and we pick out a movie. "Why are we watching a movie?"

"I don't want you to get tired of working with numbers. Best to learn a little at a time."

"Oh." Hailey says as I put the movie in the player.

CHAPTER 18

It takes two weeks before I get an appointment with the school psychologist. The rest of the class if getting ready to take the unit test on word problems and I still have not done one question.

The teacher sends me to the office and the secretary directs me into a room with a table and two chairs in it. A man sitting in one of them.

"Abby, come in and take a seat."

I sit down. "I am Mr. Newland, the school psychologist. They tell me you have a problem with math."

"Just word problems."

"And what is your difficulty with word problems?"

I tell him the story of that horrible day in Mr. Richter's class. In as much detail as I can remember and the result. Then I sigh.

"Why does being called Abigail upset you so much?"

"My birth mother's name is Abigail. The judge took away her parental rights but she and her father keep trying to kidnap me to put me to work in the family business."

"What business is that?"

"Drug dealing and prostitution. In fact, they are in jail right awaiting trial on new charges because they broke into our house to kidnap me. They hit Dad over the head."

"Abby, do you think you are to blame for your mother?"

"No, they tried to kidnap me when I was six and Dad sent me to a counselor who talked to me. I know that to my mother and her father I am not really a person but something they can manipulate for gain."

"How did your father react to what happened in your class?"

"It took me a while to explain and he said that my brain remembered my being upset every time I opened my math book. He just didn't know what to do about it."

The man nods.

"I thought not being able to do math would stop me from doing lots of things but I could still bake muffins. Then I could do the math with Roland, who Dad paid to tutor me before he understood the real problem. So I can still do math only it changed a lot of other things."

"What did it change?"

"Because Serena stubbed me at church, I got to be good friends with Hailey the next Sunday. Dad came to church and met Hailey's mom, Penny, who happened to be my Sunday School teacher. Dad and Penny got married. So now I have a new mom and a new sister."

"That is a lot of changes."

"And all since the beginning of spring break. Now I have to figure out how to get my mind to read word problems again."

"Abby, do you like your new mother and sister?"

I nod.

"Do you think life is better at your house now because your Dad met Penny?"

"Yes."

"Okay, let's try this. I want you to think about how much better your life is now. I want you to think about how you had to go through a bad time to get to now. I want you to tell yourself that it is no longer necessary to be upset about that day happened because something good came out of it. I want you to keep repeating it until you are no longer angry about what happened that day. Once you have done that, then I think you will be able to read work problems."

I went back to class and I kept telling myself that I was happy about having Penny and Hailey in Dad and my lives. That everything that happened had to happen for Dad and Penny to get married. I got back to class just as the teacher was starting the test. I took a test paper and sat down.

I looked at the paper. The words and numbers stayed in place. I wrote the test and handed it into the teacher. Then I read a story out of a school library book until the end of class. Mrs. Gates smiles at me as she hands back the papers.

"Get a parent to sign it and bring it back tomorrow."

I put my paper in my backpack without looking at it. My mark didn't matter as much as the fact that I had been able to do questions.

Dad comes and gets us from school. "The custody hearing for Hailey is today. Penny is waiting for us at the courthouse. The judge said you were both old enough to answer questions."

Penny's mother and her husband are there along with

Penny's father who sits in the wooden seats at the back of the room. We just get seated when the judge enters and we have to rise and then we have to sit down again.

"This court is in back in session."

"Abigail Hansen, come forth as a witness."

Dad leans over and whispers. "That's you, Abby-girl."

I stand up and the clerk who called out my name points to a chair. I go over to it but he holds out a Bible. "Do you swear to tell the truth the whole truth and nothing but the truth?"

"Jesus said not to swear," I tell him.

He turns red and looks at the judge. "Do you promise to tell me the truth, Abigail?" The judge asks.

"My name is Abby. I don't answer to Abigail." I tell him.

"Do you promise to tell the truth, Abby?"

"Yes."

"Then you are to sit down and answer the gentleman's questions." The judge tells me.

That's when a man seated near Hailey's grandmother stands up. "Abby." He smiles at me. "How old are you?"

"Ten."

"When did you turn ten?"

"Three weeks ago."

"Did you have a birthday cake?"

"No."

The man blinks and then gives me a half smile.

"Did you want a birthday cake?"

"No," I answer.

"Did your family do anything to celebrate your birthday?"

"We went to visit the dinosaurs," I answer. "We went for a whole week."

The man hesitates. "How does the family going on

holiday for a week have anything to do with celebrating your birthday?"

"I am the family member who likes dinosaurs. Dad promised we would go before he met Penny and Hailey."

"How do you feel about having Penny and Hailey living in your house?"

"I like them there."

"All the time?"

"Your honor." Dad's lawyer stands. "That is an unfair question."

"Abby will answer the question."

"Yes, I like them there all the time."

"Why?"

I pause. "Penny started working in Dad's office and now he doesn't have to work as many hours. Even when he does, Penny is there to talk to me. Hailey gets excited about stuff and just makes lots of things more fun. It feels safer with a second adult in the house. I don't have as many nightmares as I did before."

"You never have any disagreements with either Penny or Hailey?"

"None that we could not work out."

"Is there anything you would change?"

"Yes."

"What would you change?"

"I'd have Penny's mother and stepfather leave Penny and Hailey alone. It upsets Penny."

"What does Penny do when she is upset?"

"She goes into shock."

"So, Penny is emotionally unstable?"

"Objection your honor, Abby is not qualified to make such a judgment and neither is my opponent."

"Sustained. You do not have to say anything about that last question, Abby."

I wait for the next question.

"Has Penny ever yelled at you?"

"No."

"Does your Dad yell at you?"

"No."

"What happens when they get upset with you?"

"Dad's voice gets soft and we talk things out. Penny gets sad instead of mad. She asks me why I do things sometimes and gives me a chance to explain."

"Has she ever gone into shock while you were talking to her?"

"Only when Hailey was in danger from one of her grandparents."

"Stick to yes or no answers." The man frowns.

"Not when you use them to make the truth sound like a lie. Penny was never upset with me when she went into shock but I was in the room when it happened."

The man frowns at me.

"What did you do?"

"The first time I called Dad. The second time I asked someone to phone 911 and call Dad. At the police station, I requested a cup of water and I tried to get Penny to sip it and it spilled on her. But she hadn't quite gone into shock that time."

"You think in an emergency."

"Dad trained me in what to do. When it was just the two of us, we had to look after each other."

"No more questions for this witness your honor."

The man sits down and Dad's lawyer stands up.

"What did your Dad say to you after the clerk called your name?"

"He said that's you Abby-girl. I never answer to Abigail."

"What's all my questions." Dad's lawyer said to the

judge.

"I have a few questions for you. What is the most important benefit you have gotten from having Penny and Hailey in your life?" The judge asks.

"I got real upset in math two days before Dad meet Penny. Every time I looked at a word problem after that the words and letters broke up into arcs and sticks, then they would float on the page. The school psychologist said that if I could find something good that happened as a result of that day I could convince myself not to be upset. I used the fact that Dad and Penny got married and I had a new sister. I wrote a test with the kind of question that was giving me trouble. I answered them all with no floating bits on the page."

"How well did you do on the test?"

"I didn't look because I thought it was a win just to be able to do the questions. It's in my backpack because Mrs. Gates insist I get a parent to sign all tests."

"Can I see it?"

I get off the chair and get my backpack. I hand the paper to the judge. He looks it over and hands it back. "That's fine. You can go sit with your father now."

I go back to Dad and he takes my test paper and looks at it. He gives me a quick hug. Penny takes the paper and she gives me a hug. I return the paper to my backpack.

"Hailey Whitfield."

Hailey comes and has to promise to tell the truth.

"Hailey, are you happy living with Ted and Abby?"

Hailey nods.

"Please use words."

"Yes."

"And you think they are happy living with you?"

"It was Abby's idea to have a big party to celebrate

Mom and Ted getting married."

The man glances at his clients and frowns. "When is this party?"

"In a month."

"Why so long?"

"Ted insisted that the guests needed time to get the invitations and plan to come. He bought us each new clothes. Ted wants to hire a caterer so Mom can enjoy the party without having to worry about the food."

"Do your mom and Ted share a bedroom?"

Hailey frowns. "They each have their own bedroom."

"Have you ever seen them hold hands or kiss?"

"I have seen them hold hands. And they spend a lot of time talking to each other."

"Hailey, would you like to get to know your grandmother?"

"No."

"Why not?"

"Mom gets upset every time grandmother and especially grandmother's husband get mentioned. She never used to get so pale and have to go to the hospital. She used to work and keep house for grandfather and never get sick."

"If your mother is sick then you need someone to look after you."

"I have Mom, Ted, and Abby. Ted doesn't make Mom pay rent or buy groceries like my grandfather did. Ted and Mom share the cooking and cleaning. Ted takes the time to help me with my homework and Abby is a good friend. Best of all no one is trying to take me away from Mom. I love Mom and want to stay with her."

"You used to call your mother, Penny."

"Until Abby showed me that I didn't have to be ashamed of Mom. Mom's a kind person and a good mother. That's more important than what kids call me or what busybodies whisper behind Mom's back." Hailey squares her shoulders.

"What about your grandmother?"

"If my grandmother cared about me, or my Mom, she would make her husband go away and not let him near us."

"Why should she do that?"

"He's an evil man."

"You should not say anything you did not know for certain." The man tells Hailey.

"What I know for certain is that life is better for Mom and me now we are living with Ted and Abby. There is no reason for me to go live with anyone else. I am not going to answer any more of your questions." Hailey crosses her arms in front of her chest.

"Your honor." The man turns to the judge.

"Hailey has made her wishes quite clear." The judge tells him.

"She is only eight years old."

"That will be taken into account." The judge answers. "Do you intend to call another witness?"

"No, your honor. Like I said, my clients wish this to be dealt with as quickly as possible since they are returning home."

The judge glances at Dad's lawyer. "Do you wish to question this witness?"

"No."

"Do you wish to call any other witnesses?"

"Yes, I call Mr. William Keaton. I believe he is out in the hall."

A guard nods and brings in Mr. Keaton.

"Mr. William Keaton, will you please take the stand?"

"Mr. William Keaton, do you swear to tell the truth,

the whole truth, and nothing but the truth?"

"I do."

"Mr. Keaton, can you tell me how you know Penelope Whitfield?"

"Been a friend of the family and a fellow church member for years. I remember Penny from when she was a baby."

"Has she ever been emotionally unstable?"

"No. She has had some hard things in her life but she has always been of sound mind."

"What about the incident at the computer camp?"

"She was pushed into that by the malicious dealings of her mother. The woman lied to me on the phone about Penny leaving town. I had vouched for Penny at her job when she started work. Since I did not think Penny still needed the job, I did not stop a chain of events that got Penny fired. Penny had reason to be upset and then those two showed up and made a big scene. They tried to get Hailey to leave with them which was kidnapping. This case is just the latest example that shows they care nothing for Penny."

"Penny tried to work for you."

"The job was too physical. Penny was used to office work. She almost killed herself for two days before she admitted that she couldn't handle it anymore. I hold no ill will towards Penny." "Your honor, that is all the questions I have for this witness."

The judge glances at the other lawyer.

"Mr. Keaton, you are a friend of Penny's father."

"Actually, I went to school with Kimberly. I met her ex-husband through Kimberly. We are not close friends."

"Yet you phoned his house."

"Looking for Penny. I make it a habit to check in with people once I vouch for them so I know if trouble is on the horizon. I resigned from the board of the community center over Kimberly's lies. I was not at all happy with the outcome."

"Penny had moved."

"Not away from town nor she had quit her job both of which Kimberly insisted was true."

"Have you and Mrs. Renfue ever had differences of opinions?"

"Probably, but nothing so bad that I did not believe her lie until Penny told me she had been fired."

The lawyer glances towards his clients. "Did you not accuse Mr. and Mrs. Renfue of child abuse?"

"What I said was that there was a stronger family resemblance between Hailey and her step-grandfather than one would expect from no blood relation. Penny was eleven or twelve when Hailey was born and Penny had been forced into a court-ordered visitation with her mother for six months the previous winter and spring."

The judge frowns and takes a good look at Hailey and then at her grandmother and her husband. "Objection your honor, the witness is speculating."

"Actually, he is just stating verifiable facts." The judge answers. "This court will recess until this accusation is investigated. For now, this court rules that Hailey Whitfield is to live with Theodore and Penelope Hansen."

Dad hugs Penny. Penny and Dad. They hug both Hailey and me. Dad's lawyer cautions them that this case is not over.

"I am taking my girls home tonight. That is reason enough to celebrate." Dad puts an arm around Penny's shoulders. We walk out of the courtroom together.

"It was kind of you, Abby, to say that Penny and Hailey were the reason you could get over your math problem." Dad's lawyer says.

"It's not nice," I shake my head. "It is the truth you can ask Mrs. Shelby at my old school, my teacher, Mrs. Gates, and the psychologist. Dad told me never to lie to police or in court."

"People might believe you should be angry."

"Why? Penny saved me from Mrs. Snow at the computer camp by hanging on to me. She also kept me safe when Dad ended up in the hospital because my mother and grandfather broke into the house."

"What about at the police station?"

"Penny was worried about Hailey. Dad would have been just as upset if it had been me."

Dad's lawyer thinks about this for a minute. "Ted and Penny are lucky that you are so level headed."

"I am lucky to have both of them too. Hailey too."

"I think I agree with Abby." Dad says and kisses Penny on the cheek. "We have to keep my girls together."

"Theo, what are you doing?" A police officer has Mrs. Snow with her hands cuffed behind her back.

"I am taking my family home." Dad answers. His arm drops to Penny's waist.

"You have to save me. Talk to the judge."

Dad pauses. "I will testify against you and I hope the judge makes sure you never have control over another boy again."

The woman's jaw drops open. "The judge refused bail. I have to go to jail."

"The Bible warns that bad company corrupts good morals. I think you need the jail time to think abut your choices." Penny tells Mrs. Snow as she wraps her arms around Dad's waist.

Dad kisses Penny on the lips.

"You really hate me."

"My bedroom door was locked, Mrs. Snow. You had

the only other key. You made the supper that drugged me. Think about it."

The woman pales. "Abigail threatened me."

"I think your behavior is going to make that difficult for the judge to believe." Dad says and turns back to Penny. The policeman drags Mrs. Snow off.

"Are you okay?" I ask.

"Yes, Abby-girl. After all, this time, I think I am finally okay." Dad kisses Penny again.

Hailey looks at her mother. "Are you okay?"

Penny looks at Dad. "Better than I have been for a long time." She kisses him.

"The custody battle isn't over." Dad's lawyer reminds them.

"Neither is the business of Abby's mother and grandfather but if we wait until it all ends to be happy, we will have wasted too much time." Dad answers.

A man comes up to us. "Which is Judge Stephen's court?"

Dad's lawyer points, "But he has dismissed for the day."

"There was a call from the police on the church answering machine. I need to talk to someone about the custody case involving Mr. Renfue."

"I will show you to Judge Stephen's office." Dad's lawyer tells the man.

Dad heads us toward the door. Mr. Whitfield stops us. "You know what Kimberly will have her lawyer twist everything you say. She can be very persuasive."

"Is that why you never even tried to fight her?" Penny asks.

"Her father left her money. She thought she deserved better than a mechanic."

"I don't want to hear your excuse." Penny answers.

"All I want is Hailey. That's all I ever asked."

Dad's lawyer comes back. "New evidence, Judge Stephen wants you back in the courtroom."

We go back inside and sit down. The other lawyer is there, but Penny's mother and step-father are not. Mr. Whitfield sits at the back of the room.

"All rise."

We stand up.

The clerk announces the judge and we get to sit after he takes his seat. "This court has obtained further evidence regarding Mr. and Mrs. Renfue from his former church which dismissed him for crimes involving children. In the light of this evidence, I award permanent custody of Hailey Whitfield to Theodore and Penelope Hansen. No visitation or other rights shall be given to Kimberly Renfue. Case dismissed."

Dad's lawyer leans over. "Now you can celebrate."

ABOUT THE AUTHOR

Rosalyn Marie Francis was born and raised in Prince George, British Columbia, Canada. She is a wife and the mother of three and the grandmother of one. She has since moved to Naramata, B.C. She like writing, reading, researching and gardening.